LEAD SECURITY

*Rogue Security and Investigation Series
Book Three*

By Evan Grace

LEAD SECURITY

Copyright © 2018 by Evan Grace.
All rights reserved.
First Print Edition: September 2018

Crave Publishing, LLC
Kailua, HI 96734
http://www.cravepublishing.net/

Formatting: Crave Publishing, LLC

ISBN-13: 978-1-64034-439-6
ISBN-10: 1-64034-439-X

No part of this book may be reproduced, scanned, or distributed in any printed or electronic form without permission. Please do not participate in or encourage piracy of copyrighted materials in violation of the author's rights. Thank you for respecting the hard work of this author.

This is a work of fiction. Names, characters, places, and incidents either are the product of the author's imagination or are used fictitiously, and any resemblance to locales, events, business establishments, or actual persons—living or dead—is entirely coincidental.

DEDICATION

To my author friends:
Thank you for creating stories that allow for the perfect escape.

Chapter One

Harley

As I pull into the driveway of the blue and brick ranch-style home, I smile when I see the "Sold" written in red across the For Sale sign. I've never owned anything in my entire life. After shutting my car off, I grab the manila envelope that holds the paperwork and keys as well as my pet carrier and climb out. I'll come back for my other stuff in a bit.

When I unlock the door, I step inside and look around. The furniture looks great, and it's exactly what I picked out. I had it all delivered here as soon as I closed on the house. I do a quick walk-through and everything is exactly where it should be, which makes me happy. My office is in the back with an unhindered view of the backyard and all the flowers growing along the fence.

The desk is cherry wood and cost me some major dough, but when I first saw it I *knew* that's where I wanted to create my stories. I've been writing stories for as long as I can remember, and when I published my first two books I didn't expect them to blow up—but they did. It was slow going at first, but I was happy to at least sell one copy. But then my sales started skyrocketing every week.

In no time I was paying off my debt, student loans, and credit cards. When I started looking for houses I wasn't picky, but it had to have an office space that faced something pretty to look at.

I open the sliding glass door and step out onto the back deck, and then down the stairs. I walk around the flower beds, taking pictures of the flowers so I can take them to the garden center and someone can tell me what they are. Deep voices coming from the backyard next to mine have me turning to see the men they belong to.

One guy has brown hair and a leanly muscled body—he's holding a little girl in his arms. The other gentleman has a mixture of blond and gray hair, and when he turns so I can see his profile, I quickly swallow the drool that begins to pool in my mouth. He's got to be the most beautiful man I've ever seen. His face lights up when he grabs the baby's foot, and she squeals at him.

I watch as the little girl lunges for him, but he catches her with practiced ease. What is it about men and babies that makes women go crazy?

"Hi." I jerk and see that I was obviously staring at them. "You okay?" the younger one asks.

"Y-Yes, sorry, I just moved in. I'm Harley." I walk toward the fence and both men meet me there. I hold out my hand.

"I'm Reece, and the little cutie is my daughter, Charlotte—Charlie for short. This is my father-in-law, Jack." He shakes my hand, and then the one named Jack looks at me like I've pissed him off somehow. Reluctantly, he takes my hand in his.

It's probably best not to tell him that when he shakes my hand, I feel a zing that travels up my body. He'd run as fast as he could and never look back.

The sad, unfortunate story of my life: No one ever sticks around. The first one to leave was my mom. She died when I was five. My dad couldn't deal with her being gone, so he dropped my older brother and me off at our maternal grandmother's house and then disappeared. We never saw him again.

Things started looking up until I turned twelve and my brother became a monster. He stole money from our grandma, started using drugs, and by the time he was fifteen, he was in jail for making meth with a buddy of his. He's been in and out of jail ever since, but I had to cut him out of my life. Our relationship wasn't good for my mental health.

My grandma died from a stroke right after I turned eighteen. I was working at the time, and had I been home, I could've called an ambulance and they could've stabilized her. Instead, she died alone.

Likewise, romantic relationships for me have been few and far between—I'm no virgin, but with the opposite sex I have no luck. For my first real relationship he cheated on me…and married the girl he cheated with. Last I heard they were at kid number three. For the other serious relationship I've had, he was just there one day and gone the next. He ghosted right out of my life.

After that I just didn't see the point in trying anymore. That's why I write: because the relationships in my books always end in happily ever afters, and in reality that just doesn't always happen.

Jack drops my hand like it's covered in cooties. I'm not stupid—I can take a hint. "Umm...well, it was nice meeting you." I turn, hustling back up the stairs and going into the house.

After eating a quick sandwich I head outside and begin to bring boxes in. I'm carrying the last of the boxes when I trip—over my own two feet, I'm sure. The box on top goes flying, and I go down hard on my knees, crushing the box still in my arms.

I turn over and sit on my ass, and when I look down, my knees are torn to shit. The blood is coming through the fabric of my jeans. Of *course* I have rips in my knees now, which sucks because these were my favorite pair of jeans.

I bury my face in my hands and will the tears burning my eyes to dry up. Once I've got myself in check I take a deep breath, stand up, and limp to the box that flew off of the other one. I bite my lip to keep from crying as I bend down to pick it up.

"Jesus," I hear someone mutter behind me. Closing my eyes, I pray that I'm just hearing things and no one is there. "Give me the box and get inside." I open my eyes to see Jack staring at me with these intense eyes, intimidating me.

He doesn't even give me a chance to hand him the box—he just grabs it from my hands and moves toward the door. I pick up the one I smashed and follow slowly behind him. He sets the box down against the far wall and then rolls his eyes as he takes the other box from my arms.

"T-Thank you for your help," I tell him as he sets it down on top of the other box.

In the corner of the living room, I open the door to the pet carrier and pull my lilac-colored Lionhead Lop bunny, Fifty, out. He snuggles into me as I cradle him to my chest.

"What the fuck is that?"

Jack comes walking over to me and lifts Fifty right out of my hands. "*Hey!* You could at least *ask* to hold him. He's a Lionhead Lop bunny. He's super smart and is already litter-trained. While I write he lies on a little bed on my desk."

"What do you write?" His voice is deep, and just rough enough to be *really* fucking sexy.

This is always awkward, but I've learned not to be ashamed of what kind of books I write. "I write erotic romance under the name Eva Steele. 'Harley Sanders' didn't really scream erotic romance."

I look at Fifty, who seems to be content in Jack's hand as the large man scratches right behind his ear. He loves that.

"Are your books like those Fifty Shades books?" I shake my head because really, they're not. "Tell me about them."

I walk over to a box labeled *books* and use the box cutter to open it. I grab the first book in my series. It's called, *Love Me, Always*. It's the enemies-to-lovers storyline with a twist: They were "boyfriend/girlfriend" when they were little, but she moved away.

I hold it out to Jack. "Here, this is my first book.

Read it, and I'm seriously okay if you don't like it." We trade—he takes the book, and I take my bunny back.

"Thanks, I'll check it out." He moves toward the door. "Make sure you clean up your knees so they don't get infected."

"Um...okay. Thank you." I stand to the side of the door so he can't see me, and to my horror he walks to the garbage bin outside of Reece's garage and tosses my book inside. I gasp, apparently loudly enough for him to hear because he lowers his head and reaches back inside to grab it.

I don't bother watching the rest. How could someone be so *mean*? I put my heart and soul into these stories, and for someone to take my hard work and throw it in the trash...it *hurts.*

After slamming my front door shut, I slump against it. Jack doesn't like me, so who cares? He doesn't live next door. I'm sure it won't be hard to ignore him.

***

My doorbell rings, pulling me from my laptop. I pick up my phone and see that it's lunchtime. Fifty is passed out on his bed so I just leave him snoozing and head to the front door. I look out the window and see Delilah and Charlie.

It's been two months since I've moved into my home, and when Delilah and I met I knew immediately that I liked her. It's hard to believe that her and Jack are father and daughter because she's so sweet, and...well, he's a grade-A asshole.

Opening the door, I greet them with a genuine smile. "Hey, guys! Come on in." Delilah knows the drill and hands me Charlie as she steps inside. "Hi, pretty girl." The sweet little cherub squeals and gives me a smile that melts my heart. "Not that I'm not happy to see you, but what brings you by?" That's when I realize that Delilah's got a backpack over her shoulder.

"There's a problem at the office that I need to take care of. Can you watch Charlie? I should only be gone a couple of hours."

I've watched the little princess a couple of times and she's the easiest baby...of course, she's the only one I've ever really been around. "Of course I can. I hit my word count already for the day."

"Thank you so much. I'm sorry to just hop on over here and put you on the spot."

I hold up my hand. "Stop, it's no problem. She and I can take Fifty out into the backyard to play." Delilah is obsessed with my bunny, but with a new puppy at home it'd be too much to get one of their own.

"That'll be fun. Where is my favorite, furry little baby?" she asks.

"He's sleeping on his bed in my office." Before I can blink, the blonde disappears down the hall, returning with Fifty in her hands while she strokes his head. My little baby is a sucker for any sort of attention. He's gotten used to Charlie's noises, too, so when she sees him and emits a high-pitched squeal he doesn't even move.

Delilah kisses Fifty's head and then sets him down on his little blanket on my couch. I hand

Charlie back to her momma and smile as I watch Delilah snuggle her daughter to her chest—or as close as she can with her pregnant belly. "You be a good girl. I love you." Charlie smiles at her mom and babbles in two-year-old speak. A wave of sadness washes over me. What would it have been like to grow up surrounded by my mother's love? She's been gone so long now that I can't remember anything about her. Did she love us? Did she hug and kiss us all the time?

I plaster on a fake smile, taking Charlie back when Delilah hands her over. Luckily the little girl loves me and doesn't cry when she sees her mom leaving.

When the door shuts I look down at Charlie. "Should we go play outside?" She claps her hands together and squeals...*loudly.*

Outside for our second time, Charlie walks on her chubby little legs as I hold her hand in one of mine and Fifty's leash in the other. We walk along the flower beds and stop in front of the butterfly garden. I had no clue the treasure I had in my backyard until I took the pictures into the garden center and they told me what everything was. The employees also told me how to take care of them.

I'm by no means an expert, but at least I don't feel like I'm going to kill them. I get down on my knees next to Charlie and scoop up Fifty in my hands.

"Uba!" Charlie shouts. I'm not sure what that means, but she bends down and touches her lips to the top of my baby's head.

"Do you see the pretty butterflies?"

She leans into me, hugging my arm, and squeals. "Yes!"

"Where's my nugget?" a male voice calls from the front yard. *Ugh...why is he here?* I close my eyes and take a deep breath before I stand up.

"Hey, Jack," I say as he walks into my backyard.

Charlie squeals. "*Pa Pa!*" She runs to her grandpa as fast as her little legs will take her. An ache blooms in my chest when I watch his whole face change as he holds out his arms to his granddaughter. The man is beautiful in the rugged, manly way, but when he's giving attention to Charlie, he's breathtaking.

"Hey." He finally acknowledges my existence. "Reece took Delilah to the doctor. She was having cramps. I told them I'd come get Charlie."

"Oh gosh, I hope she's okay."

"Reece is freaking out. Delilah swears it's just Braxton Hicks. Anyway, I told them I'd take Charlie back to my place for the night." He scoops Charlotte up in his arms. "Thanks for watching her."

He turns, and just like that, he's gone. "Fucking dick," I mutter under my breath.

Chapter Two

Jack

One Year Later

For the past year, I've been in *hell*. Every time I visit my daughter and grandbabies, I catch a glimpse of the petite, auburn-haired, green-eyed beauty, and my cock aches to be near her, to be inside of her. It'll never happen because I followed my dick once and it led me to Becky—granted, I'll never regret it because I got Delilah out of the deal, but yeah, it's *never* going to happen again.

Of course my daughter immediately became friends with Harley, and my granddaughter loves her. It's not unusual for Harley to be over there watching or helping with the kids when I stop by. Yes, okay, I *may* stop by more than I need to, but it's purely a "look but don't touch" situation. Touching is forbidden.

Fuck, speaking of touching…I haven't had sex in almost three years. God, that's pathetic, but I've been too busy getting my company up and running. Everything that happened with Delilah and her having my grandbabies also has kept me busy.

Anytime I decide to jerk off, Harley is the queen of my fantasies. Plus, now that I've read her books—and yes, I've bought every single one…they're almost better than porn—I have lots and lots of material to serve as inspiration for my pleasure.

I picture her as the heroine every single time. Then when I'm around her, I just want to touch her. Apparently I like to torture myself. Let's not forget, though: She's thirty-two and I'm forty-three and a grandfather. I'm just too old for her; she probably wants marriage and babies, and I don't.

Don't get me wrong—I love women and I love pussy, but I don't love the drama that usually follows them. Uncomplicated is what I've enjoyed…easy breezy.

After mowing the grass and trimming the bushes around my porch, I put everything away and head inside to shower. My daughter and son-in-law are having a cookout today, for no other reason than to get everyone together. Plus I can spend some time with my grandkids, Charlie and my namesake, Jackson.

When I get out of the shower I throw on jeans, a t-shirt, and motorcycle boots. It's a nice night; I might as well take my bike. I can't wait until my little Charlie girl is big enough that I can take her for rides.

On my way out to the garage, I grab my helmet. When I pull up into Delilah's driveway, the front door opens and my son-in-law steps out with my grandson in his arms. I couldn't have found a better husband for my daughter if I'd picked him myself.

"What's up, brother?" Reece hands over Jackson, and I hug my baby boy to me. "Your granddaughter's in a timeout right now."

I smile, because she's definitely giving her mom and dad a run for their money. She's a good girl—she's just *very* stubborn and tests her parents all of the time. "What did she do this time?"

"She decided to steal her momma's lipstick and draw all over her room, and then decided to draw on her brother." Reece pulls up Jackson's t-shirt, and I can see the faint marks on his belly. We head inside, and I set Jackson down before he crawls toward the kitchen.

I find Charlie sitting in a little chair facing the corner. When she sees me, she smiles like she's not in timeout. "Papa, I twouble."

It takes a lot for me not to go pluck her out of the chair and smooch her face, but my daughter would kick my ass if I interfered. "I see that, my little nugget. Come give me hugs when Mommy lets you up."

"Otay!" She smiles.

"Hey, Dad." I kiss my daughter's forehead and follow them through the house and out the sliding glass door. I spot Harley right away, sitting next to Erik's fiancé, Shayla. She glances at me and then turns away...*good.* It makes it easier to resist her if she avoids me.

By the time food's on, the kids are all fit to be tied. Shayla and Erik's oldest, Grant, helps Charlie and Carrie and Egan's oldest son, Leif, up the stairs from the yard. We get the kids all set up, and then we all sit down to eat.

I'm not sure how it happened, but somehow I end up seated next to Harley. She ignores me while talking to everyone else. I really haven't been the nicest to her.

"Harley, what story are you working on now?" Delilah asks.

Harley's cheeks turn a light shade of pink. "I'm plotting a couple of different things right now, which is usually what I do while I'm waiting for edits to come back. I'm doing my first book signing next weekend—it's at the Barnes and Noble at the mall. Will you guys come?"

My daughter, forever the cheerleader, starts clapping and bouncing up and down. "We'll *totally* come. Right, girls?" She looks at both Carrie and Shayla, and they nod their heads in agreement.

Conversation starts to die down as the evening wears on. Harley left a little while ago, and my granddaughter is asleep on my lap. Reece keeps offering to take her, but I shake my head every time, refusing to give up my little nugget.

Delilah joins me a few minutes later after putting Jackson to bed. "She loves her papa."

"Her papa loves her." Bending down, I place my lips on her curly brown hair. "Thanks for dinner."

"Of course." Delilah looks at me closely. "Have you ever thought about getting married again, or having more kids?"

She's honestly never asked me this before. I shrug. "I haven't. After your mom, I just never let myself get close to someone again. She sent me a letter after that first year...I had no plans to read it, but my curiosity got the best of me."

"What did it say?" Delilah leans forward and puts her hand over mine.

I tilt my head back and close my eyes. "Sweetheart, you don't need to know. It's not important." Nausea had pooled in my belly when I read Becky's words. We created the beautiful woman in front of me, and she said she never wanted her. It was all to trap me, to mess with me, but then the reality of motherhood didn't appeal to her.

Delilah interrupts my thoughts. "Dad, it's okay. I know she never wanted me. I'm okay with that. I've come to terms with it. All I know is that I'm not her. I love my kids and will *never* make them feel like they were mistakes." She lets go of my hand and strokes Charlie's hair back from her sweet cherub face.

"You may have come to terms with it, but I haven't. It really fucking sucked to read her words. She should've given you to me. Yes, you would've been with your grandma and grandpa, but they would've shown you love."

We head inside, and I take my Charlie girl upstairs and tuck her in. Both kids are asleep, so I decide to take my leave so my daughter and son-in-law can enjoy the rest of their evening. When I head out to my bike and straddle it, I hear Harley's garage door open. Seconds later, her car pulls out of the driveway.

When she takes off down the street, I start my

bike, pull out of the driveway, and follow behind her before I can stop myself. I know she sees me, and I pull in behind her at a little pub called Duey's that's two blocks away.

She climbs out. "Are you following me?"

"Maybe...are you meeting someone?" I move toward her, crowding her against the side of her car. Harley stares up at me, and her green eyes sparkle under the light of the parking lot. "Answer me, darlin'." In my head I know I should step back, hop on my bike, and ride away, but I can't.

Harley crosses her arms over her chest, which of course draws my attention to her breasts, but I force my eyes to stay on her face. "It's not like it's any of your business, but no, I'm not meeting someone. I just felt like I could use a drink, and I didn't have anything at home." She scoots around me and heads toward the door, with me trailing behind her like a fucking dog.

The light is dim inside, and the place is damn near empty. I sit down next to her at the bar and signal the bartender over. Harley orders a spiced rum and diet and I order a beer. She doesn't talk to me at first, and I watch out of the corner of my eye as her lips wrap around the red straw.

"How's your bunny?" Fuck, I'm lame.

Her laugh is soft and melodic, and goes right to my dick. "He's fine. How was the rest of the party?"

"Good." I pull out my phone and bring up my photo app. Holding it out to Harley, I show her the picture Delilah took. It's my nugget asleep on my lap. I know I constantly bombard people with pictures of my grandkids, but I love them to pieces. I mean come on, I delivered Charlie myself.

"Awww...she's so adorable. You're very lucky to have such amazing family. I love those little munchkins."

I take my phone back and take a drink of my beer. "I *am* lucky. It's still sometimes hard to believe that I almost lost both my girls." I don't dare tell my daughter that I still occasionally have nightmares about that day. Delilah doesn't know that I saw her heart shatter that night while she held her newborn daughter in her arms and looked to her mother for any semblance of love. The fucking bitch wouldn't even look at her.

That is why I'll never be in another relationship. "What about you?" I ask. "Are you and your family tight?"

Her whole demeanor changes; her eyes focus on her drink, she's picking at her fingernails, and a wave of sadness comes off her that makes me want to pull her into my arms. Instead I change the subject. "I've read some of your stuff." I never planned on telling her, but I don't want her to be sad.

"You have?" Harley sounds genuinely surprised, but why wouldn't she? I was an asshole the day we met, and when I left her place I know she saw me throw her book in the garbage. It was a dick move, but considering the attraction I felt it seemed safer to be a dick in order to keep her away from me.

"I have, and you're fucking talented." I love the shade of pink her cheeks turn. "What made you decide to write?"

Harley turns toward me, and our knees are almost touching. I hate that she won't look me in the eye. I reach out and grip her chin, tilting her face up until I can see the vibrant emerald color. Her pink tongue pokes out, moving back and forth over her lower lip...I want to nip it.

"Tell me what made you decide to write."

She narrows her eyes at me. "Are you *always* this bossy?"

"Of course I am. You don't lead a team of alpha males without being bossy at some point." I let go of her chin and grab my beer for another swig.

"I'm seriously shocked that you read my books, considering..." She grabs her drink and sucks down some of it. "You didn't have to throw it in the trash. You could've just said no when I gave it to you."

I rub a hand over my hair. "It was a dick move, and I'm sorry."

"Thank you for saying that. I do want to ask you a question." Harley sucks down the rest of her drink. She sets the glass down and then asks me point blank, "Why don't you like me? Since the day we met, you've treated me like I was nothing."

I open my mouth to speak, but she slides off of her stool so she's between my legs. She grabs my face, and the next thing I know her lips are on mine. Harley licks the seam of my lips, and I open to her and quickly take possession of her mouth. My dick is harder than it's ever been, and if I don't get control of myself I'm going to end up fucking her here on the bar.

But before I can pull her closer...she's gone, the door to the bar shutting behind her. In a daze, I shake my head and turn back toward the bar. *Motherfucker*.

Chapter Three

Harley

"Why did I kiss him?" I mutter as I pour a cup of coffee. It's been three days since I kissed him and I can't stop thinking about it. His flavor exploded on my tongue, his lips were firm, and it made me ache in a way I've never felt before…which in turn caused me to run.

Jack obviously didn't feel anything because he didn't follow me out, and I haven't seen him since. It's not like I care, but now it's going to be even *more* awkward around him. "Harley, you're an idiot." *Great*, I'm talking to myself now.

With my coffee in hand, I head into my office. To stay on track I have a set schedule, obviously with a little flexibility. In the morning while I "wake up," I go through emails and social media. I pick up Fifty and snuggle him in my arms. He's the laziest animal I've ever seen. In seconds, he passes out. As I scan my emails, I notice a couple from my website.

The first is from a fan that's just discovered my books. I can't help it and smile wide while I read her email. I shoot her a quick response back, thanking her for writing and saying that I'm so glad she loves my stories.

I open the second. My body tenses as I read the words.

> Ms. Steele,
> I thought I should inform you that I find your writing very offensive to women. God will punish you for your sins. Repent before it's too late.
> Yours in Jesus,
> Martha

Ugh, I hit delete and roll my eyes. This isn't the first time *"Martha"* has emailed me or messaged me telling me that what I write is wrong. I ignore and delete every one. It's not worth it to let it get to me. Back to the task at hand, I post a teaser from my upcoming release on all of my social media sites and all of the links I have ready.

Once that's all done, I carry Fifty out into the kitchen with me, where I grab a banana and Fifty's leash. It's a beautiful, warm morning, and when I step outside I see there are butterflies flitting around my butterfly garden. Once my bunny is on his leash, I walk him with me toward the garden.

The week before, I bought a bench and placed it in front of my butterfly garden. I love to come out here and just get lost in my thoughts. Sometimes if

I'm stuck working on a difficult scene or I'm blocked, I'll come out here and let my mind clear, and it gets the creative juices flowing. While I eat my banana I feed Fifty a couple of little pieces, which the pig happily gobbles up.

I watch a couple of butterflies flit around and smile. A familiar squeal has me turning on my bench and watching Charlie running toward me with Delilah walking behind her with Jackson in her arms. The little cutie pie runs right to me. I set Fifty on the ground between my feet and scoop her up onto my lap.

"Hey, Harley, sorry to bug you, but I need a *huge* favor." The blonde sits next to me and settles Jackson on the bench between us before she reaches down to scoop up Fifty.

"Sure, what's up?"

She sighs. "I'm pregnant…or at least I'm pretty sure I am. I've got an appointment at my OB/GYN, and then I have to go kick Reece's butt."

"Oh wow, I thought he got the old snip, snip." I make the motion of scissors with my fingers.

"He did, he just refused to take his sample in to see if it worked, which *obviously* it didn't. I hate bugging you, and I feel like I ask you to babysit all of the time." Delilah kisses Fifty's head and lets Jackson kiss/drool on his head after her.

"You know I'm always happy to watch them, but I wish I could see you kick Reece's butt."

"Butt!" Charlie yells, and then hops off of my lap and walks over to the flowers. I love how she's so gentle when she checks them out.

Delilah shakes her head as she looks at her

daughter with soft eyes and the sweetest smile on her lips. A wave of sadness washes over me because I'm never going to have that—I'll never be someone's mom. At thirty-two, you'd think I'd be over my abandonment issues, but I'm not and never will be. I'll never allow myself to truly be close to someone because I'm never going to be left again.

While I put Fifty in his cage, Delilah takes the kids back over to her place. It's easier for me to watch them there. I grab a bottle of water and head on over. Since she knows I'm coming I don't even bother knocking. I just step inside, and their labradoodle, Jinx, greets me at the door. "Hi, boy." I scratch him behind his ears and then follow him into the living room.

Charlie is on the floor brushing the hair of her doll. Delilah brings Jackson out. "They've already eaten, but can have a snack in a little bit. I just changed his diaper."

I take him from his momma. "Go, I've got this." She gives me a smile. Quietly, she grabs her purse and disappears.

Charlie doesn't mind her mom leaving, but Jackson gets upset. I use the power of distraction to get him calmed down, and sure enough, he stops crying.

The kids play together, with Charlie only getting irritated a few times. After they play for a while, I get them set up in the kitchen with some Goldfish crackers and sliced bananas—watching as they munch happily on their snacks.

When I'm wiping their faces off, I hear the front door open. "Where are my little nuggets at?" I roll my eyes—what is he doing here? I was hoping I could keep avoiding him.

"Papa!" Charlie runs toward him while Jackson tries to lunge from my arms. Luckily I know the little boy well so I had a good hold on him.

I get that familiar flutter in my stomach when I watch Jack smile at the kids. He picks Charlie up, hugging her to his chest and kissing her cheeks until she squeals. "How's my girl?"

"Hawey's hewe." She points to me.

Jack's eyes meet mine, and that stupid flutter intensifies. "I see that," he says to her while looking at me. "Where's Del?"

God, I love his voice. It's slightly rough, and makes my brain short circuit. "She had an appointment. She'll be back in a little bit."

He comes toward me and holds out his arms to Jackson. "Come here, monkey man." I hand him over to his papa and can feel his eyes on me, but I avoid them.

While Jack plays with the kids, I read the e-book I started the night before. I'm not sure how much time passes before I feel little hands on my knees. I set my e-reader down and smile at Jackson. "Hey, buddy." He gives me a drooly, toothy grin as he stands up, holding onto me.

Jackson has a short attention span and gets down to spider man crawl across the room to his papa. "Charlie, do you want to help me pick up the toys before Mommy gets home?"

While picking up, I feel Jack's eyes on me, but I ignore him. Delilah gets back while Charlie and I are still tidying up. I watch father and daughter share a moment when she tells Jack that she is, in fact, pregnant again.

I'm filled with a sense of longing. I would've loved for my father to love me like that, and I know I shouldn't let it bother me because it's been so long that I barely remember my father. I *certainly* don't remember my mom, but there's this loneliness that is constantly there.

Ugh, I shake those thoughts off because thinking about that now isn't going to help me. I tell them goodbye, making my escape as quickly as possible. When I'm safely inside my home, I flop down on my couch and then lie on my side, curling in on myself.

As much as I love spending time with my wonderful neighbors, I'm alone—I've got no one. I get up, shaking off those thoughts. I head into my bedroom, changing into some cut-off sweats. I put my hair up in a knot. Heading into the backyard, I stick my earbuds in and get down in my flower gardens, pinching off the dying or dead parts.

I don't know why it's so relaxing, but I can lose hours out here. When I finish up, I head inside to shower.

***

I pull into the parking lot of Barnes and Noble and my palms begin to sweat. This is the first signing I've done, and I'm scared to death that no one will come. I did do a lot of advertising for it. I asked bloggers to share, and have shared with my readers on social media. Out of my trunk I grab my banner and the container with all of my swag: bookmarks, candy, pens.

The manager, Michelle, greets me at the door. "Hi, Eva—we're so glad you could come today." I've learned that it's better just to tell people my name is Eva, instead of Harley. It causes too much confusion.

I hold out my hand. "Thanks for having me. I'm so excited to be here."

She leads me to a table that has my books displayed on top of it. Michelle takes my banner for me and sets it up so it stands tall off to the side of my table. I'm nervous because there doesn't seem to be anyone waiting to see me. Granted, the signing doesn't start for twenty more minutes.

I lay out my swag on the table and grab a couple of pens and a marker out of my bag, laying them out on the other side of me. After that's done, Michelle leads me to their little coffee shop and I grab a vanilla latte. I head back to my table and sit down behind it. I pull out my phone and check in on Facebook so anyone who follows me knows where I am.

My nerves kick in as I see the clock getting closer and closer to one o'clock. There are a few people here, but they're milling around. I drink the rest of my latte and let Michelle know that I'll be right back.

I use the bathroom and wash my hands. I check myself in the mirror and sigh. Working from home has its advantages, but when I actually get out I try to at least do my makeup and hair. I pull my lip gloss out and dab it on my lips. This color, candy apple red, is a lot more daring than I'm used to. Normally I stick to the clear gloss, but when I woke up I decided I wanted to be a little daring.

I grab my powder and swipe it over my nose, around my mouth, and my chin. In the mirror, I give myself a once-over. I decided to wear a pair of gray skinny jeans, a pair of peep-toe black booties, and a light hunter green gauzy t-shirt with a white cami underneath. I turn to look at my backside and sigh. "I *really* need to start working out more," I whisper.

I'm just like every other woman: overly critical of my body. My boobs are too small, my hips are too wide, and my butt too big. Oh well—I can't do anything about it right now. I take a deep breath before grabbing the door handle and stepping out into the hall.

When I reach the table, I see a couple of women standing a few feet away from my table talking to each other. Michelle walks up and smiles. "Don't be nervous. People will start filtering in soon."

As soon as I sit down, the two women waiting come toward me with big smiles. They've both read my books, and we start chatting. It makes my heart swell to see them both so passionate. They both buy my latest release and I sign it for them. After posing for pictures, I hug them both and watch them walk out.

For the first hour it's sporadic, but then a line starts to form. I sign books, e-book covers, and bookmarks and pose for pictures. Everyone is nice, and so it's easy to talk. When I look up, watching the girl whose book I just signed walk away, I spot Delilah, Shayla, and Carrie standing toward the end of the line.

They wave wildly and then give me the thumbs-up. It takes about twenty minutes before they reach me. "I know someone famous." Delilah says it like I'm a movie star or something.

I come around and hug the three of them. "Thank you so much for coming."

"We wouldn't miss it." Shayla gives me a huge smile. "Plus Erik loves it when I read your books." She wiggles her eyebrows at me.

"*Ewww*…gross," Delilah says while covering her ears. "I don't want to hear that. He's like my brother."

"Yeah, but he *is* pretty hot," Carrie adds.

Shayla holds up her hands. "No more talking about my hot fiancé. My hormones have made me crazy enough already." She rubs a hand over her swollen belly.

They each grab the books they want to buy, and I get busy signing them while they chat about their kids. Even after losing my mom and then essentially my dad, I still wanted children. I wanted a loud, loving family that was close. Until the day I realized that it just wasn't meant to be. I'm green with envy, and I shouldn't be—I'm happy for my new friends, but I wish I was able to join in their conversation.

The four of us pose for a couple of pictures, and then I say goodbye.

I look at the clock and see that my time is up. I've had a lot of fun, and even made a new fan when the woman stopped at my table and asked me about my books. After we finished talking, she bought my first series.

I stand up as I begin clearing off the table. Moving around to the front, I look at what books are left. Michelle comes over to me. "You had a nice turnout."

"I did! Thank you again for having me." She heads back toward the front, and I hear a throat clearing behind me.

I'm sure the look on my face is comical when I find Jack of all people standing behind me. Of course the asshole looks hot as fuck in dark washed jeans and a dark gray t-shirt that molds to his chest and shows off his muscular arms. "H-Hey. What are you doing here?"

Jack runs a hand through his hair. "I was in the neighborhood and remembered you said you were signing books today. How'd it go?"

I'm struck speechless. I know I look ridiculous as my mouth opens and closes. I take a deep breath. "I-It went well. Thanks for asking."

"Good. Will you sign one for me?" He walks up to the books still sitting on the table and grabs one off of the top. "This one."

I take it from him and sit down. I pick up my pen and open the front cover. This one was my favorite to write. It's about two co-workers who don't get along, and then after a drunken night they sleep together. She ends up getting pregnant, and they try making their relationship work. It's not an easy journey, and it's pretty angsty, but they do get their happily ever after.

After I sign it, I hand it to him. "Thank you for coming. That was so nice of you."

His whole demeanor changes and it's like he just

shuts down. "I'm not nice—remember that." He walks away leaving me confused and irritated. One thing I know for sure is I'm done trying to be nice to the asshole.

I signal Michelle to come grab the books that are left and quickly pack my stuff—making my escape before he comes back.

Once I'm home, I take everything into my office and put it away. I pull Fifty out of his cage, letting him hop all around the living room while I clean his cage and feed him. I grab myself a glass of wine. I head out to my swing and have a seat.

I sip my glass of Riesling and watch the birds fly around, singing to each other. Why did Jack bother coming if he was going to turn the asshole on? I swear I think he just hates me and loves giving me whiplash with his mercurial mood.

Lord knows he's been avoiding me since the night I kissed him—not my finest moment, apparently. Kissing him awakened my slumbering libido, and now I've got sex on the brain constantly. It's only been a week since it happened, but I can't stop thinking about my lips on his, or the way he took complete control of the kiss.

I've only ever had two lovers, and they were long-ish relationships. It's been four years since the last time I had sex, but honestly I have better orgasms when I masturbate. Lane and John were nothing to brag about, either. Of course Lane said I was a cold fish in bed, and that's why he cheated. Then it made me tense up with John, so the sex was awkward and underwhelming.

But today is a new day. What if I went out,

picked up a man, and had sex? Just a one-time thing, and then I'd never have to see him again? I review the pros and cons in my head over and over. *Ugh, thanks a lot, Jack, for making me crazy and confused.* I stand up and head inside, making the decision to just go out and see what the single men situation looks like.

In my bathroom I plug in my flat iron and then head into my bedroom. Two years ago, I bought my first little black dress, but I've never had the courage to wear it. I pull it out of the closet and look it over. Back in the bathroom I take a quick shower, rushing through shaving my underarms and legs. This impulsive idea makes me glad that I wax down below so I don't have to worry about doing any shaving there.

I smooth lotion all over my body and then slip into an emerald green silk bra and panty set. I may not go out, and I may not always wear a bra, but when I do, I want something pretty. I put my robe on as I head into the bathroom to do my makeup.

I'd love to say I give myself smoky eyes and dewy skin, but instead I go for the "less is more" look, opting for some mascara, a little bronzer on my cheeks, and red-tinted gloss on my lips. I flat iron my curls and then pin my bangs to the side.

I slip into my dress, which is form-fitting and hits me right above my knees. The bodice is slimming and gives just a hint of cleavage. The sleeves are capped with ruffles around the edge. I can't do heels so I slip on a pair of black wedges. I grab my iPad and Google bars that are within twenty minutes from my place. On Yelp I find a whiskey bar that looks promising. It's eight o'clock and hopefully it's not too busy. If it is, I'll stay for a drink and then come home. I pop a mint in my mouth, grab my car keys, and lock up the house.

I sing along to the radio as I drive across town. I'm a terrible singer, but I'll do anything to quell the nerves. I sing along to Heart while I pull into the parking lot of the bar and feel myself relax when I find there aren't a ton of cars here.

Chapter Four

Jack

"Don't worry about us. You guys deserve a night away," I tell my daughter as my son-in-law drags her out of the house. They're going to see Pink downtown, so I rented them a suite for the night. "I've got Elizabeth on speed dial."

Delilah runs toward me and throws her arms around my neck. "I'm not worried. I just hate leaving them, but I love you and thank you for staying with them."

I kiss her forehead and smile down at her. To me she'll always be the little blonde girl with pigtails who'd make me spin her round and round until we'd fall to the ground. Her little giggles were the balm to my soul. It's hard to look at her now and see that she's a grown woman with a family of her own.

"Reece, take care of my daughter." They wave from their SUV and pull out of the driveway. I close and lock the door behind me. In the living room,

Charlie is glued to *Peppa Pig*, and luckily she was oblivious to her mom and dad leaving.

"Hey, my little nugget, I'm going to check on your brother, and how about Papa makes some dinner?"

I laugh and shake my head because she holds out her hand in a shooing motion, which I know she gets from her mother. Upstairs I find my namesake standing up in his crib. He reaches for me as soon as he sees me. I scoop him up and snuggle him to my chest. My boy loves me, that's for sure.

While I change his diaper, we discuss the Bears' chances of making it to the Super Bowl. He babbles away in his secret baby language. Once my boy is cleaned up, I carry him downstairs. I hear Jinx barking from the backyard so I let him in.

My eyes go to Harley's backyard, hoping to catch a glimpse of her—stupid I know, but there's just something about her that pulls me in and makes me want to make stupid decisions…the kind of decisions that left me with a crazy ex-wife who was going to steal my grandbaby and sell her.

***

Jackson's crying so hard it's almost a scream. The kiddo went down for the night a few hours ago, and when he started screaming it scared the shit out of me. I ran upstairs and found he'd overflowed his diaper. He was sitting in the middle of his crib screaming bloody murder with big fat tears rolling down his cheeks.

I took him into the bathroom, got him cleaned

up, and dressed in fresh pjs. He cried the whole time. Now we're downstairs and I've tried rocking him, bouncing him, and singing to him, but he's still inconsolable.

Headlights flash across the living room and I look out the front window to see Harley pulling into her driveway. I open the front door, and she must hear Jackson's screaming because she looks toward us. "I need help," is all I say and she comes rushing over.

"What's going on?" Harley walks up the steps. "Jackson, what's the matter?" She plucks Jackson from my arms and walks right by me into the house.

"He's been like this for about the past hour. If you've got him, I've got to go grab his bedding. The kid shit up his back, his front, and all over his crib."

She hugs the baby to her chest and kisses his forehead. I watch her place her hand on his forehead. "Do you have a thermometer? He feels warm."

I run upstairs and grab it. Harley takes it from me and runs it over his forehead. When it beeps, she looks at the display. "He's got a low-grade fever. Do they have some children's fever reducer?"

"Let me check." Up in the nursery I find the ibuprofen and take it downstairs to her. I'm ashamed to admit I'm freaking out a bit. I've been deployed, I've seen and done things I wish I could forget, I've dealt with a psychotic ex-wife and delivered my granddaughter, but now...now I feel like I'm failing my grandson because I didn't realize he was sick.

Harley reads the label, and then brings me my

boy. "Take him while I get his medicine ready." She disappears into the kitchen and returns with a little syringe-looking thing with purple liquid in it. "Hey, little man, I need you to take this." She grabs Jackson gently by his cheeks, puts the tip of the syringe in his mouth, and slowly gives him the medicine.

Half of it he spits out, but she just scoops it up with her finger and brings it to his lips. My grandson obviously knows a good thing when he sees it because he lunges for her, gripping her hair and burying his face in her neck as he whimpers.

Eventually, it's four in the morning, and I'm exhausted and half delirious. Harley and I have taken turns getting up with Jackson—or I should say, *sitting* up with him. His fever went down, but the poor kid is restless. Right now I'm at one end of the couch while Harley is asleep on the other end, facing the back with Jackson lying in between.

While she snores softly, my grandson plays with the ends of his hair and drinks his bottle of Pedialyte. I don't know what I would've done without her help tonight. She didn't once act like it was bothersome for her to be here, and even when he had an explosion that got all over the sexy as fuck dress she was wearing, she just smiled, ran home to get clean clothes, and then took a shower in the hall bathroom.

When she was in the shower I threw her dress and Jackson's pajamas in the wash, hoping that the material wouldn't be ruined. I'd *really* like to see her in it again.

I texted Reece an hour ago just so he'd know

what they were coming home to. If I know my daughter, they'll be home by eight if not sooner.

Luckily every time I've checked on Charlie she's been passed out in her princess bed that I bought her for her third birthday. Jinx is oblivious to all the drama going on, sleeping tucked into Charlie's side.

By the time seven o'clock rolls around, Jackson is finally sleeping, but only if he's on Harley. We tried to move him, but he screamed his head off. I got them situated on Del and Reece's bed surrounded by pillows—just in case, but the kid hasn't moved since.

I watch the two of them sleeping curled up together and I feel a foreign feeling in my chest. I rub at it, trying to make it go away, but I'm interrupted when I hear that sweet little voice.

"Papa!" My girl is always happy when she wakes up.

I put my finger in front of my lips, and she copies me. "Brother is sick, and finally sleeping. Can you be a big girl and be quiet?"

She nods and then disappears into the bathroom, sitting on the toilet with the door wide open. When she's done, she washes her hands. "Don't forget to brush your teeth."

While she does that, I take Jinx out, and she joins me in the kitchen a few minutes later. "What do you want for breakfast, Nugget?"

She taps her chin like she's thinking, which is something Reece does. In looks she's all Del just with dark hair, but she acts just like her daddy. "Waffles!"

Charlie's on her second helping, and I'm

LEAD SECURITY

downing my third cup of coffee when the front door opens...knew it. I greet my daughter and son-in-law, and she doesn't look happy. "Dad, why didn't you call us? We would've come home last night."

"That's exactly why I didn't call you. I didn't want you to have to come home. Harley and I had it handled."

Delilah freezes, and then looks at me. "Harley helped?"

"Yeah, we were an hour into his meltdown when she pulled into her driveway. She came over and helped. We finally got him to sleep, but he'd only sleep on her, so they're on your bed. I hope that's okay."

My daughter wraps her arms around my waist. "Thank you for taking such good care of my babies. What's going on with him?"

I tell her what happened while Reece sits with Charlie in the kitchen. Upstairs we stop in the doorway of their bedroom and watch Harley and Jackson sleep. "It sounds like his ears again. This is the second ear infection he's had." Jackson hears his momma's voice because his eyes pop open and he crawls off Harley, waking her up.

Harley sits up looking dazed, grabs Jackson, and crawls off the bed. Delilah takes Jackson and hugs him to her chest. My eyes go back to Harley—why does her sleepy look turn me on so much? I turn away to avoid looking at her and getting an erection in front of my daughter.

The girls talk quietly as they follow me downstairs.

In the kitchen I grab my coffee and pour Harley

37

one, which she gladly accepts. "How was Pink?"

"Dad, it was amazing. Wasn't it, Reece?" My daughter bends down and kisses her husband's temple.

Reece smiles up at her. "It was great, baby."

I'll admit I wasn't happy when I learned what went down between these two, especially with Reece being so much older than Delilah, but over and over he's proven to be an amazing husband and amazing father.

"Well I'm glad you guys had a good time." I wrap my arms around my daughter's shoulders and kiss her forehead.

Harley stands up. "I'm going to head home and take a nap." She bends down and kisses Charlie's cheek, and then that feeling in my chest comes back, especially when my little nugget giggles and wraps her arms around Harley's neck. She kisses her cheek and leaves syrup lip prints behind.

Harley doesn't even wipe it off—she just bops Charlie on the nose and says goodbye to Reece and Del.

"Thanks for helping Dad with Jackson."

"It was my pleasure," she says before I hear the front door open and close.

I stare in the direction she just left in, feeling eyes on me. I look down to see Delilah and Reece both staring at me. "What?"

"Nothing…nothing at all." She smirks, and I shake my head.

"I'm going to go crash. Let me know if you need me for anything." I kiss my grandkids and then my daughter before I head out to my truck, but instead of climbing inside and going home, I walk over to Harley's.

I ring the doorbell and contemplate leaving the entire time I wait for her to answer, but when I hear the deadbolt flip and the door open I know it's too late…or at least that's what I keep telling myself.

"What's up, Jack?" My eyes rake over her, and my dick twitches in my jeans. She's in a red cami and little bootie shorts that are light gray. *Were her legs always this long?* "Do you want to come in?"

I don't answer her—I just step through the doorway into her living room, shutting the door behind me. "Come here," I say softly, loving that she doesn't hesitate. When she stops in front of me, the scent of lavender fills my nose.

I reach out and tuck an errant curl behind her ear. "Thank you for helping last night."

Her cheeks turn a light shade of pink. "It was my pleasure. I was happy to help." Harley stares up at me and licks her lips nervously. I don't miss the way her pupils dilate.

Every muscle in my body pushes me to reach out and grab her—to take her, to claim her, but is that what I do? No, of course not—instead, I grab her gently by her shoulders and move her back away from me.

"See ya 'round." I walk out and hop in my truck. I don't miss my daughter watching me from her front window.

I need to get laid—finally break the celibate life I've been living, and maybe then I'll no longer feel that invisible pull toward Harley. She's the type of trouble that I don't need. Been there, done that, bought the t-shirt. I'm not saying she's like Delilah's mom, but I just can't go through that again.

***

"Yeah, Friday at nine sounds good. I'll make sure Egan's there," I tell our sales rep for our security equipment. They've got new cameras that are supposed to be top of the line, but I don't order any of that stuff until Egan looks it over.

"Great Jack, I'll see you then."

I hang up, add the meeting to my calendar, and then send Egan an invite. He's still here so I'm not surprised that he answers me right away that he'll be at the meeting. I grab the signed invoices from my desk and take them down the hall to Del's office, which is occupied by Shayla today.

I come to the door and find Erik down on his haunches, both hands on Shayla's swollen belly, and he's talking quietly to it.

I knock on the doorframe. "Sorry to interrupt. Here are those invoices. How are you feeling, sweetheart?"

She shoots me the biggest smile while her fiancé continues to talk to and rub her belly. "I feel great Jack, thanks." Shayla points at her belly. "We're having a boy." They're only a few weeks from her due date.

"That's fantastic news. Just remember they said *Charlie* was a boy. They can be wrong." The moment my Charlie girl slid free from her momma and I saw she was a *she*, I'd been shocked, but so happy.

Erik stands up and holds up the picture. "Look, he's showing off the goods." Sure enough, the kid has everything on display.

I slap him on the back. "That's great news, brother." I move around the desk and pull Shayla into my arms and kiss the top of her head. "Congratulations. What does Grant think about it?"

Shayla had been married before and the son of a bitch was abusive. It took her son, who was three at the time, witnessing one of his father's assaults on her before she finally left him. Her boy was understandably skittish around men, but Erik's seemed to have turned that around.

Now Erik, the reformed womanizer, and Shayla are getting married. They have a hard road to travel, but they're all settling into life together, and we're all happy for them.

"Grant's excited. He and Erik have had talks about big brother responsibilities." She smiles up at Erik. "*Both* of my guys are excited."

I leave them and head down to my office. I'll do some research on a case I'm working on and then head to the gym before I finally head home.

I pull my truck into my garage and climb out as the door shuts. Inside, I toss my keys and my wallet on the breakfast bar. I head into my bedroom and strip off my sweat-soaked t-shirt and shorts before heading into the bathroom.

I let the water flow over my body, relaxing my sore muscles. I rub my hand over the scar on my left hip from the shot that made me decide to end my military career. Most days there's a little ache, but when I work out it can sometimes get worse, causing me to walk a little stiffer when I first get up.

It's hard to believe that it's been six years since I took the bullet. When I thought I was dying, my life flashed before my eyes. Everything I saw was about my daughter: regrets for leaving her with her mother, leaving her when I was deployed, and regret for not fighting harder to protect Delilah.

I push those thoughts away because they only get me upset, and they don't change anything. Instead, my thoughts flash to the beautiful auburn-haired thorn in my side—images of her with my grandson snuggled against her chest bring forth thoughts of her holding *our* child that way.

"Fuck," I growl before I turn the water off and step out of the shower. I quickly dry myself off before wrapping my towel around my hips and heading into the bedroom.

I sit down on my bed and grab my laptop. I type in the address of the porn site I visit when I need to get off, but instead of hitting enter, I backtrack and Google Eva Steele. When her beautiful smile pops up on the screen, my cock immediately gets hard.

I get settled on my stack of pillows and wrap my hand around my dick. Images of her flashing me that smile while she rides my dick flit through my mind while I begin to pump up and down. *Fuck,* I haven't done this in a while; I can already feel that tingle at the base of my spine.

I close my eyes and imagine flipping her over, slapping that gorgeous ass of hers as I pound into her from behind. If I think real hard, I can hear her moan my name, and then I come all over my hand.

I clean myself off with my towel, shut off my laptop, and climb under the covers. *I need to get fucking laid*, is my last thought before I fall asleep.

Chapter Five

Harley

I stretch my arms above my head as I finish my marathon editing session. For the past forty-eight hours I've barely slept, working round the clock to get my edits back to my editor. I glance at my desk and shake my head; wrappers, pop bottles, and cups line my desk—the proof that I've barely moved. But edits are done now, so I can relax the rest of the day.

I pull the garbage bag out of the little can in my office and start throwing away the trash. Once that's done, I open the windows to air out the room. It's not like it smells, but the air is just a little stale.

I carry the trash out the back door and throw it into the can. The sun is almost blinding, but I tip my head back. The warmth seeps into me, and I sigh. I glance over at Delilah and Reece's place when I hear Charlie's little girl giggles.

I smile when Reece comes into view with his daughter on his shoulders. "Fasser, fasser Daddy," she squeals in her little girl voice.

He starts jogging around their yard in circles, her little hands in his and her little brown pigtails bobbing up and down behind her. That sense of longing fills me again, but I push it down.

I step back inside before he catches me staring and gets the wrong idea. I grab Fifty out of his cage and let him hop around while I clean his litter box. When that's all done, I take him with me into my office and place him on his bed. I send my manuscript back to my editor and check my email.

There's a couple from readers, and I quickly answer them. There's also one from *Martha*, but I delete it; I'm not in the mood to hear how horrible I am. I see a couple of emails from the dating site I signed up for in the spur of the moment the other night. Being lonely is probably not the right reason to join, but when I had gone to the bar to look for a man, it had been an absolute disaster.

The only guys who hit on me were either young and hammered or old and sleazy. I didn't even finish the drink I ordered. Instead, I went to a little diner by the bar and had coffee and pancakes while I read on my phone. When I got home and before I got out of my car, I heard a baby screaming.

I enjoyed helping Jack with little Jackson, but was so exhausted when it was over. After I went home and Jack showed up things got weird between us and I thought he was going to kiss me, but instead he left and he's avoided me ever since.

I know I should just forget about the infuriating man, but I can't. I'm drawn to him in a way that scares me…and exhilarates me. He's definitely shown me time and time again that he's not into me. When will my dumbass get with the program and just think of him as a friend—one that doesn't really even like me?

I pull up the emails from the dating site: One is a welcome email, and one has instructions on how to log into the app to see my matches. I grab my phone, download the app, and then after entering my email and password, my account pops up. The notification tells me that I have two men possibly interested.

The first is Peter: a thirty-four-year-old single father. I click on his picture, and he's cute. He's got light blond hair, and it looks like brown eyes. He works for the Chicago Cubs. The second is Jonathon, a forty-year-old professor at Loyola University. He's got no kids, and doesn't want them.

He's very handsome, and reminds me of a more polished version of Jack—*nope*, not going there again. That man is no longer going to monopolize my thoughts.

Before I lose my nerve, I type out a quick response. I respond to Jonathon.

Harley: Hi Jonathon, I'm not sure what to say but it appears we're a match. I don't know how this works, but if you'd like to talk just message me back. We can exchange emails-Harley

I tip my head back and stare at the ceiling. When

did this ache form inside me? I've always been at least content with my life. I've never felt this lost, but maybe living next to Reece, Delilah, and their family has made me realize what I've been missing most of my life.

They're a beautiful family, and it's clear how much they love each other. My grandma used to tell me stories about my family before my mom died. My mom played piano and her and Daddy would sit together and sing for my brother and me. We'd dance around the living room together for my grandma and grandpa to watch.

The four of us were inseparable, and then it all fell apart. My dad was so heartbroken when he lost my mom that he couldn't handle us and took us to our grandma's.

I've often thought about hiring someone to find my father—for the sole purpose of knowing if he's okay. I've thought about finding my brother, but with his record and history of drug abuse I can't take the chance that he's still a mess and getting on his radar.

I plug my phone into the charger and then strip out of my clothes on the way to the shower. Sometimes when I get lost in my work I skip the daily hygiene—it's scary, I know.

I take my time scrubbing myself from head to toe, washing and conditioning my hair twice. When I'm done I feel human again. After moisturizing my face and body, I blow dry my hair and then throw it into a knot on my head.

After throwing on some athletic shorts and a t-shirt, I head back into my office, grab Fifty, snuggling him close before I put him in his cage, and grab his food and fresh water.

I hear my phone ping in the other room, and I grab it out of the office. My heart rate speeds up when I see it's a message from Jonathon.

***

I never thought another person could be so freaking boring, but Jonathon is the worst. Things were great when we messaged each other, and then texted. We've done the texting thing for a couple of weeks, and he seemed like a really nice guy, but then we decided to meet.

Delilah came over earlier and helped me pick out an outfit, although she seemed to not be very enthusiastic about it, and she wouldn't say why. To keep it casual I'm wearing gray tailored shorts, a white tank top, a short-sleeved emerald green cardigan, and black ballet flats.

"Are you sure this is a good idea?" she'd asked.

"It's just coffee," I'd told her, but she still didn't look convinced. I gave her the guy's name, the name of the coffee shop, and promised to call when I was home.

She'd looked at me closely, and then sighed. "Okay, but seriously if you get any bad feelings you call me, and I'll send Reece to rescue you."

Now I'm listening to Mr. "I'm the smartest man in the universe" drone on and on about every award he's won, and how he's the head of his department. We've been here for a half hour and he hasn't stopped talking. He's such a good-looking man, and there is nothing wrong with confidence, but this guy *loves* himself.

Over texts he seemed generally interested in me, but now…nothing. I sip my latte and feign interest while he talks, and talks, and talks, and fucking talks.

"So tell me about yourself, Harley. What do you do for a living?"

"Um…well I'm an author. I write romance novels." The minute his nose crinkles I brace for the snide comments, and he doesn't disappoint.

"So you write porn? Nice."

I ball my fist and feel my hackles rise. "It's not porn, it's romance stories with sex. There's nothing wrong with love stories."

"Ha! Love stories? They give women unrealistic expectations."

I stand up. "You know, obviously you didn't read my profile—otherwise you would've seen that I put right on there that I write romance novels. Then maybe you wouldn't have wasted my time, or yours."

I head out to my car feeling extremely disappointed. I'm tempted to cancel my account and say forget it. I could've said I did something else, but I refuse to lie about it. I'm not ashamed of what I write. I love the beautiful tales I tell, and yes, the sex is raw, dirty, and very descriptive, but that's what I love about writing it.

Maybe I'll give the other guy a chance, or see if anyone else is a match. When I reach my house I find Jack and Reece standing on the sidewalk with Charlie riding her hot pink motorized motorcycle.

When I get out of my car, I see Del's out front on their steps with Jackson and she waves me over. "How was your date?"

"It was terrible." I reach her and hold out my hands to take the baby and snuggle him to my chest. "He spent most of the time talking about himself. Then he asked me what I did for a living, so I told him because I'm not embarrassed. He basically told me I write porn, and I give women unrealistic expectations."

"Oh my God, what did you say?"

"I told him he would've known that had he actually read my profile and that he wasted my time."

"Well...maybe next time you'll have better luck." She gives me a quick hug.

We sit on the front steps while the men follow behind Charlie as she rolls down the sidewalk. "I don't know. We'll see. I wanted to get back out there, but I just haven't had any luck so far. Fifty's the only man I need in my life...or this little cutie pie right here." I kiss Jackson's chubby cheek, and then blow a raspberry on it until he squeals.

We're both quiet for a moment, and then Delilah surprises me. "What do you think of my dad?"

I freeze. Does she know? "Umm...what do you mean?"

She looks at me closely, and flashes me a smile. "I see the way he looks at you. I've seen the way you try to avoid looking at him. It's funny; when my dad called earlier and I told him you were out on a coffee date, he came right over, and he's been out front looking at your house every couple of minutes."

I shake my head. "I don't know what you think you've seen, but he doesn't like me. Most of the time he acts like he can't wait to be rid of me."

Delilah grabs my wrist and leans in. "My mother did a number on him. I honestly haven't seen him date since I've been in Chicago."

"Aren't daughters supposed to hate the women who come into their father's lives?"

She laughs softly. "Nah…I just want him to be happy, maybe give me some brothers or sisters, and have the love of a good woman. I think that woman could be you."

I know my mouth is hanging open right now. It even opens and closes, but nothing comes out. "How do you know it's me?"

"Just a feeling I get, especially when you're near each other. I think you might be just what each other needs. Plus we love you, our kids love you." She holds her hands up. "No pressure and I know he can be a grump, but just think about what I said."

Luckily she drops it. She and I decide to take Jackson and Jinx for a walk. I grab the stroller out of the garage. While she goes into the house to get the dog, I get Jackson all strapped in. Delilah comes out with Jinx on his leash, then we walk.

***

I grab my salad and carry it into the living room, and turn on the TV. I pull up *True Blood* on my Amazon Fire Stick: my latest binge-watching treat. I've seen it before, but it's been a while. I've thought about writing a paranormal romance because I love to read them. The rest of the year is pretty booked up, but that's on the agenda for next year.

I grab Fifty and snuggle up with him on the couch. I feed him plain pieces of lettuce while I eat my salad. I finish eating and place my bowl on the coffee table, curling up on my side absently stroking Fifty's soft fur.

My phone pings and I grab it off of the table. I have another match on that dating website. With a sigh, I toss my phone back on the table. I'm not in the mood to look—Delilah's words run through my mind.

She can't possibly want me with her dad, but she's under the wrong impression that he likes me. I won't lie, as much as I don't want to—I have a crush on the man. My doorbell rings, pulling me from my thoughts. I stand up and look out the window—it's a UPS driver.

I smile when I open the door. "Here you go, ma'am, sign right here." He holds out the little device for me to sign.

I take the package from him and close the door. "Fifty, what is this?" Sometimes I forget when I order swag or paperback books. I look at the return address and it's a P.O. Box. I take the box into the kitchen, grab a knife, and open it.

It's some shredded paper. "That's weird." I dig through the box, and it's empty. That's when I notice a sliver of paper looks like it has color on it.

It takes a few seconds to realize it's one of my books—actually, it appears to be *several* books. I dig through the scraps, looking for a card, a note…*something*, but come up with nothing. I bury both hands in the box, grabbing wads of shredded paper, and begin to cry.

All of my hard work, and someone just destroyed it. God, that hurts so much. I let the papers in my hand go and pick up the box. I don't even care that I have tears running down my face as I step outside and walk down to the curb where my garbage bin sits.

I flip the lid open and tip the box inside until all of the paper is emptied out. I wipe angrily at the tears as I march back up to my front door. "Harley?" *Shit,* I really don't need his crap right now.

I keep my back to him. "Hey, Jack." I quickly step inside, but I feel him step in behind me. I close my eyes to get myself straight, then turn to look at the man. "What's up?" Trying to act casual, I give him a smile.

"Why were you crying? What was in the box?"

"It's really none of your business. Go away." I turn from him and feel him follow me into the kitchen.

"Whatever it was upset you. Tell me what was in the box." He crowds me until I'm against my refrigerator. "What. Was. It?"

I try to shove him away, but he's like a freaking rock. "It was one or more of my books, and the asshole completely shredded them."

"Did they leave a note?" I shake my head. "What about the return address?" Jack's voice is softer, gentler, than he's ever used with me before.

"It was a P.O. Box." I look down and realize my hands are still on his chest. I go to move them, but he puts his hands over mine, holding them there. "If you're wondering why I was crying, it's because they took my hard work and destroyed it like it was nothing, and I was pissed."

Before I can react, he palms the back of my head and pulls me toward him. My arms automatically wrap around his waist. I begin to cry again as he comforts me. "I could j-just scream I-I'm so mad."

"Has something like this happened before?"

I start to shake my head, but then I remember the emails. "A woman named Martha, she emails me sometimes. She tells me I'm a *sinner*. I should repent…yada yada yada. It's harmless."

"If she sent the books, she knows your address. Darlin', is your real name and address listed anywhere that a reader could get ahold of?"

"I don't think so. No one knows me by my real name. You guys are the only ones who know that I'm Eva."

"Do you have the emails?"

I shake my head. "I didn't see a reason to keep them."

He pulls back and looks down at me. My fingers itch to stroke his square jaw that's covered in just enough scruff. "Promise me if you get emailed again you keep it and let me take a look. People are crazy and not everyone can be trusted."

I nervously lick my lips, and I don't miss the way his eyes land on my mouth, watching my tongue wetting them. I nod. "I promise."

"Good," he whispers just before his lips are on

mine. It's a surprisingly soft kiss that makes my toes curl, and my pussy clench. I let him set the tone, and he doesn't disappoint. He increases the pressure and coaxes my mouth open. Our tongues dance together, and I moan against his lips.

I grip his t-shirt at his sides as I tip my head to allow him deeper. A warm feeling spreads through me, and I want to be as close as I can to him. Jack must be able to read my thoughts because he wraps an arm around my waist, hugging me to him. I don't miss his erection that's pressed against my belly.

All too soon Jack ends the kiss. He cups my chin and strokes his thumb back and forth across my lower lip. "Fuck me, you're pretty," he whispers, and then leans down to kiss my lips again before pulling back. "Have dinner with me tomorrow night?"

"Okay, I'd like that." I'm trying to remain cool when all I want to do is jump up and down screaming, but he's been so hot and cold with me.

"I'll be here at seven." He leans down until his breath tickles my lips. "I'd really love it if you wore that black dress."

I nod, and he grabs my hand and then walks me toward my front door. He kisses me one more time, and then he's gone—just like that.

I can't help but wonder if I made a mistake saying yes to him. Is this going to be one of those times where he acts like he's into me but then pushes me away? Only time will tell.

Chapter Six

Jack

I pull my Expedition into my garage, kill the engine, and hop out. I've got an hour to get ready for my date. Fuck, I can't remember the last time I went on a date. Hell, I think it was shortly after Becky and I got divorced. I was too fucked up to really give myself to someone.

I swore I was over it, but when everything happened with Delilah and Charlie, it brought it all back to the forefront. I swore I was planning on staying away from Harley. She's made me think about things I never planned on thinking about ever again, but the moment I saw her crying in her front yard I knew I couldn't stay away from her any longer.

My daughter has been hounding me since last night asking questions. Earlier today she came into my office and tried to pump me for information. She's definitely my daughter, and she'd make a hell of an interrogator, but I told her nothing.

I know she's been worried about me, and I've tried to convince her I'm fine, but my daughter is living on her happy cloud, which makes me glad. Her life wasn't always the best, and as much as I know it's not my fault, a part of me will always feel like it is, or it was. But now that Delilah is on her happy cloud, she wants everyone else on it with her.

I can't believe I have three grandbabies...well, two and one on the way. Their house is chaos, but they don't care. As her father I made so many mistakes, but seeing what a wonderful mother she is makes me feel like I'm not such a failure.

Shaking off those thoughts, I hop in the shower, and when I'm done I wrap a towel around my waist. I grab my shaving cream and proceed to shave my face. I slap on some aftershave my daughter convinced me to buy. I grab the jar of hair shit and run my fingers through my hair.

In my bedroom I throw on a pair of my dark jeans, a fitted black t-shirt, and my black motorcycle boots. A thought hits me: I can't *really* pick her up—I don't want Delilah to get the wrong idea. This thing with Harley could go really wrong, and I'd hate for my daughter to lose her friend, and it seems that Harley doesn't have a lot of people in her life, either.

I'm an asshole, I know this, and there's a huge possibility that I'll hurt Harley—not intentionally, but it could happen. I don't want to destroy their friendship because I'm a dick. No, I can't *not* go pick her up—now that would be a dick move.

I shove my wallet in my back pocket and grab my keys before I head out.

Pulling into Harley's driveway, I don't miss the curtains move in my daughter's living room. I want to shake my head and laugh, but instead I pretend that I don't see her or Charlie peeking out the window. *God, I love my girls.*

When I reach Harley's door I hit the doorbell and wait for her to answer. Always watchful, I look up and down the street, but I don't know what I expect to find. Harley doesn't know I took the box out of her trash. I have a buddy on the police force that's going to check it for fingerprints and then run them in the system.

The front door opens, and I turn to look. Harley is standing there, in front of me, and I feel my dick twitch in my pants. She's fucking *stunning*. Her auburn hair is pinned back, my guess at the base of her skull, and her makeup is soft except for the red gloss on her lips.

She's wearing *the* little black dress and black strappy wedges. Harley pushes open the screen door. "Hi, Jack."

I step through the door, and her sweet, floral scent wraps around me. I watch her walk toward the kitchen, my eyes immediately going to her perfect ass. I would give my left nut to have her cheeks in my hands.

I follow behind her like some lovesick fool. She fills up a water bottle and then I watch her bend over as she sticks it in her damn bunny's cage. That thing...I'll admit it's cute, and my granddaughter loves it, but what does a bunny *do*? It can't protect you. What purpose does it serve, except to be snuggled?

When she stands up I place my hands on her hips and fit my front to her back. At first she holds herself stiff, but then she relaxes against me. I lean down and put my lips to her ear. "You are fucking gorgeous."

"T-Thank you." She turns in my arms. "You look handsome."

I reach behind her and quickly pull the pins out of her hair until it tumbles around her shoulders. "I like it better down," I tell her as I sift my fingers through the soft strands. The scent of coconut hits my nose, and I know it's her shampoo. "We better go or we're never going to leave." She looks at me with confusion, but then she must realize what I'm talking about because her eyes widen, and she begins to nod.

I let her go, and grab her hand before leading her outside. We're silent on the way out to my SUV. I open the door for her and help her inside, and again I feel eyes on us. "Don't look now, but we have an audience."

Her eyes immediately go to my daughter's house and she laughs softly. "If they're trying to be sneaky, they're really bad at it."

I close her door and walk around to my side, giving my daughter, son-in-law, and granddaughter a wave. Shaking my head, I climb in and we head out, and out of the corner of my eye I watch Harley wave to my family as they watch us from the window.

"Where are we going?" she asks.

"Do you like Chinese? There's a great restaurant that's kind of a hole in the wall, but their food is fantastic."

"I love Chinese food."

I park half a block down from Ying's. I discovered this place while I was doing surveillance and became addicted to it. It's a little family-run business, they have no sign and do no marketing, but the place is always packed.

I climb out, moving around the front to help Harley down. I lace my fingers with hers as we head down the street to the red door. As soon as we step inside, the smells hit me and make my mouth water.

"Oh my God, is it wrong that I want to lick the air?" she says, looking up at me with a smile that takes my breath away.

I can only laugh, and it feels fucking good. I wrap my arm around her shoulders and hug her into my side. The matriarch of the Ying family, Li Liu, comes over smiling. "Hello, Mr. Mackenzie. I see you brought a pretty lady tonight." She grabs two menus and leads us to a table in the corner. "Enjoy."

"Thank you, Ms. Liu." She nods and then disappears. I pull out Harley's chair and then take the seat across from her. Ms. Liu returns with a pot of tea, and then leaves us.

I pour myself a cup of tea and lift the pot in her direction and she nods. "This is obviously a frequent haunt. It's busy, but you managed to get a seat right away."

"I was doing surveillance nearby when I discovered, and became addicted, to this place. They had a break-in a year and a half ago, and my crew installed a security system and more secure doors for them. I charged them for materials only, and at a discount. They're a busy restaurant and I'm sure they make good money, but they send a lot of it home to their family in China." *What in the hell is wrong with me? Why am I nervous?* I'm babbling about shit she probably doesn't care about.

The Yings' granddaughter comes to takes our order, and then disappears to grab us waters. "Tell me about your family?" I turn back to Harley and ask.

"Ummm...there's not much to tell. I don't really have one anymore."

That answer has me curious, but before I can ask what that means, our waitress brings our drinks out. When she leaves us, I open my mouth to ask Harley about her family, but she asks me about my grandkids. Everyone who knows me knows those kids are my everything.

"The kids are good. You've seen them in action. They wear Delilah and Reece out, but they're both always smiling." They bring our food out, and conversation is stalled while we eat, but Harley's appreciative moans are making it hard for me to concentrate.

"You're right. This *is* the best Chinese food I've ever eaten." She smiles at me and takes a big bite of her rice and vegetables. "Thank you for asking me to dinner. I was beginning to think that you didn't really like me much."

I set my chopsticks down and reach across the table to grab her hands. They're soft, and I drag my thumb across the top of her knuckles. "I'm the first to admit I'm a dick. I was attracted to you, and to be honest I didn't want to be." I shrug. "It was easier to be an asshole than admit that I wanted to get to know you better."

"Thank you for telling me that, and even though you *were* a dick, I still had a crush on you." Her cheeks turn a deep shade of pink, and she lowers her head.

"Don't be embarrassed. I like that you're into me."

Harley shakes her head and rolls her eyes. "Oh brother, you're too much."

We're both quiet as we finish eating. After we finish, I pay the check and we head out. I'm not ready to call it a night yet, and I hope she isn't, either. "Do you want to grab a drink?"

"Sure, I've got beer at my place if you want to come over." I'm frozen; I don't know what to say, but I've obviously stood here for too long because suddenly Harley's walking toward the exit.

"Harley, wait up?" I follow her out to the street. "I'm sorry, I was just surprised that you were inviting me back to your place."

"Okay, sorry." She surprises me and pokes me in the stomach. "If you weren't so hot and cold with me, I wouldn't be so sensitive."

I really like that she's honest, telling me exactly how I made her feel. "See...I told you I was a dick."

"Well, stop being one." She smiles up at me.

I grab Harley around the waist and bring her flush against me. "Come home with me?" I sweep her hair out of her face. "I've got a really nice back deck."

"Okay, sure. I'd like that."

I lean down and kiss her forehead. "Let's go." I grab her hand, leading her to my SUV.

We make our way toward my place. Before the grandkids I lived in an apartment in the city, but after, I wanted a place closer to my daughter. My house had been kind of a dump when I bought it, and the in-ground pool had been a mess.

It took about six months and a lot of work to make it a home. I pull into the driveway of my bungalow Craftsman. The siding is gray with navy shutters, and the front door is red—Delilah picked that out. All the landscaping was done by Delilah and my mom when my parents were here visiting last summer to spend time with their granddaughter and great-grandbabies. Mom and Dad moved to Florida as soon as Dad retired from John Deere.

"Wow. I really love your place," Harley says as I lead her inside. My dad, Reece, his dad, and I had gutted the place and worked with contractors to give it an open layout. We went with light beige walls and laminate flooring throughout. My daughter and Mom decorated the place, giving it an arty, but manly, look.

The kitchen and dining room are a pale yellow. The kitchen has granite countertops and a matching island. The dining room table is long with plenty of room for my grandbabies. In the corner is a highchair and booster seat.

Hand in hand, I show her around. Harley stops and picks up a baby doll sitting in a basket next to the couch. "Yours?" She strokes her hand over the brown hair of the doll.

I hold up my hands. "You caught me. I love to play with dolls."

She places it gently back in the basket. "I knew you were a dollaholic."

"*Dollaholic?*"

Harley moves to stand in front of my bookcase, looking at pictures. "Yep, I just made that word up. I bet you play dollies with Charlie, don't you?"

I step up behind her and grab onto her hips. She picks up one of my favorite pictures. It's from last Christmas and Delilah's tucked into my side with her head on my shoulder. She's got my namesake sleeping on her lap, and Charlie is sitting on mine. "Your family is beautiful, Jack."

My dick gets hard whenever she says my name, and this time is no different. "They are. Del didn't have a very good momma, but that didn't stop her from being the best." She sets the frame back on the bookcase.

"Let's finish the tour and then we'll go sit out back." I take her upstairs and show her the room I have set up for the kids. I take her into my bedroom; the walls are a grayish-white and my bed is a California king, but my room is big enough to hold it. My furniture is all distressed pine.

"Wow, that's the biggest bed I've ever seen." She walks up to it, turns around, and falls backward on it.

I walk toward the bed and fall back on it too.

Harley turns toward me and smiles. "It's comfy."

I turn so I'm lying on my side, and she does the same. "It is." I grab Harley's hand and bring it to my lips, kissing it. I want nothing more than to strip her bare and kiss every inch of her body, but I don't—instead I get off the bed, grab her, and pull her to standing. "Let's go get a drink."

Downstairs I grab us both a beer and lead her out the French doors in the dining room that open to the back patio and pool. Once I flip on the lights, I don't miss her softly said, "Wow." I follow her as she walks down to the pool.

She pulls her wedges off and sits at the top of the stairs, sticking her feet in the water. "This feels so good."

"I keep it lukewarm for the kids." I take off my boots and socks, rolling up my jeans enough to dip my feet in the water as I sit down next to Harley. I grab the beers that I'd sat down and hand her one.

I watch her throat work as she takes a drink from her bottle before I take a drink of my own. The night is quiet around us, but it's nice. I spend most of my days on the go, so it's nice to be able to just sit and *be*.

"Earlier you said you didn't have a family anymore. What did you mean by that?"

Harley looks down at her lap. "I meant that I don't *have* a family. My mom died when I was little. Dad couldn't handle it, so he dumped me and my brother with our grandma, and we never saw him again. My brother turned into a drug addict and a monster. I finally cut him out of my life, and when I was eighteen my grandma passed away, and now I have no one."

She says nothing more, just staring out across the yard. "I think I'd like to go home now," she murmurs.

I shouldn't have brought them up—I should've just left it alone. "I'm sorry." Harley just shrugs her shoulders, but I can tell she's shutting down on me. She stands up and slips her shoes back on. I grab the beer bottles and follow her inside.

As soon as I pull on my boots, we head out to my SUV. Harley's quiet while we head back toward her place. I grab her hand in mine and give it a squeeze. Thankfully she squeezes it back. I pull into her driveway, climb out, and come around to help her out.

Harley holds my hand as we walk toward her front door. "I'm sorry I ruined our night." She looks up at me, and her eyes are shiny under the porch lights.

I reach out to stroke her cheek. "You didn't ruin anything. I'm sorry about your family." I know I'm lucky to have loving family. Were we perfect? No, but I never doubted my parents loved me.

She opens her door and pulls me inside. "Coffee?" I nod and follow her into the kitchen. I sit at the table while she fiddles with her coffeemaker, and then the sound and smell hit me as the coffee begins to brew.

Harley comes over and sits next to me. "It's been a long time, and I don't know why, but sometimes it *still* bothers me. I've thought about finding my dad, to see if he's still alive. I don't think I'd want to speak to him...or maybe I would, just to get answers."

The coffeemaker beeps and she gets up, pouring us both a cup. "Do you want me to find him for you?" I ask.

Her head whips up. "You would do that?"

I grab Harley's hands, leaning forward. "If you want answers, I'll find them for you."

She grabs me by my chin, pulls me to her, and kisses my lips. Then after way too little time, Harley pulls back until our lips are no longer touching. "Can I think about it?"

"Of course. You say the word and I'll find him." Harley throws her arms around me, hugging me tightly.

She lets go of me and covers her face. "I can't believe I had a pity party on our date. *God,* you must think I'm a mess."

"Fuck, no. Come here." I pull her from her chair until she's on my lap. "Don't *ever* feel bad for your feelings." I stand her up and do the same. "I'm going to go, but I'd like to see you tomorrow."

Harley nods. "I'd like that very much. Thank you again for dinner, and I didn't get a chance to tell you, but I *love* your pool."

"How about tomorrow night I'll grill us some steaks, and you can bring your suit? We'll take a swim."

"That sounds great."

I bend down and kiss her forehead. "Pack a bag and plan on spending the night."

"O-Okay."

I shake my head. "No pressure—we could just sleep. Let's just see how the night goes."

As she walks me to the door, I tell her I'll call her in the morning. I cup her cheek, bend down to kiss her lips, then I head out.

Harley watches from the door, and after I pull

out of the driveway, I wave to her before heading home.

Chapter Seven

Harley

I hobble out to my car—okay, maybe I'm not *hobbling*, but I should've skipped the Brazilian wax and just stuck with the bikini wax. I'm not planning on having sex with Jack tonight, but you never know what could happen. I'm very attracted to him, and he's attracted to me. Honestly, the idea of seeing him in nothing but swim trunks makes me a little hot under the collar.

He wants me to spend the night, and as excited as I am, I'm nervous. What if I snore in my sleep, or even worse…fart. I stop at the tanning salon and do the spray tan/tanning bed combo. If I'm going to be in a bikini—and yes, I bought myself a string bikini that is sexier than anything I've ever owned—then I need to look my best.

When I get back home, I don't bother pulling into the garage since I'll be leaving later. I walk up to the front door and hear a certain little girl's sweet voice: "*Hawey!*"

I turn and smile as Charlie comes running over in a pretty little sundress that shows off the tan she has. "Hi, sweetheart." I squat down and she throws her arms around me. Standing up with her in my arms, I smile as Reece comes walking over. "Hi, Reece. Where are Delilah and Jackson?"

"They're napping. Charlie wanted to come out and ride her motorcycle." The smile he gives his daughter melts my heart. Did *my* dad ever look at me like that? My guess is that he probably didn't if he could just discard me the way he did.

He holds his hands out to his daughter. I quickly kiss her cheek before handing her over to Reece. "Let's let Harley go." He smiles at me. "See you later."

"Bye, guys. Tell Delilah hi for me."

I watch them talk quietly as they disappear into their garage. Inside I put my stuff on my bed, and then get Fifty out of his cage. "Hi, my pretty boy, did you miss me?"

I grab some greens out of the refrigerator and sit on the couch to feed him. He nibbles away on his snack while I turn on the TV and pull up the latest episode of *MasterChef*. As scary as he is, I've always found Gordon Ramsay incredibly hot.

Once the episode is over I clean out Fifty's cage, and then I begin to clean my house. It doesn't need it, but I'm nervous about tonight and I need to burn off some energy.

By the time I'm done, I've alphabetized the books in my bookcase and rearranged my office a little. It's only noon, and I decide to lie down and take a nap.

It's three o'clock when I wake up. I climb into the shower where I scrub and shave every inch of me that didn't get waxed. After rinsing off, I wrap a towel around myself and walk across to my bedroom. I dry off and then lather myself in my favorite cocoa butter.

Since we're just staying at Jack's, I wear a pair of khaki shorts, a red tank top over a white one, and finish off with a pair of my Birkenstocks. In the bathroom, I add light makeup to my face and decide to wear my hair in a knot on top of my head.

I grab my duffel bag out of the closet and grab a pair of boxers to sleep in and gym shorts to wear home tomorrow. I grab my contact lenses case and my glasses and sit them on top of my clothes. I grab my toothbrush and face wash and add them before zipping up my bag.

I carry the bag out into the living room, and look at the time—I need to head over to Jack's. I step into the bathroom and look at myself in the mirror one more time. "You can do this. Just be cool." *Ugh, what am I doing?*

I double-check that Fifty's fed and watered, grab my bag, and head out to my car. I'm just climbing in when I hear my name called, and this time it's Delilah. "Where are you off to?" I don't miss the twinkle in her eye.

"Ummm...I-I've got a date."

"Oh God, I've embarrassed you. I'm so sorry—sometimes I can meddle and I don't mean to. I know you're going to see my dad, and I just wanted to tell you to have a nice time." She quickly hugs me—well, the best she can with her growing belly. I watch her disappear into the garage and smile as I finish settling into the driver's seat.

I punch Jack's address into my navigation system since I don't really remember where he lives. When I finally pull into his driveway, he steps out onto the porch while I climb out of my car. When I reach him, he bends down and kisses me.

When he pulls away, I whisper, "Hi." I'm such a dork.

"Did you find it okay?" He takes my bag and then leads me inside.

"I did, thanks."

Jack disappears upstairs with my bag while I walk over to the French doors. The pool is even *more* beautiful during the daytime. I feel him step up behind me and love it when he wraps his arms around me. "I got us some filets, twice-baked potatoes, and asparagus. Does that sound okay to you?"

"That all sounds delicious. Can I do anything to help?"

He shakes his head. "It can all be done on the grill, except the potatoes. You just sit and keep me company. Would you like a drink?"

"Sure, what do you have?"

I watch Jack go to the refrigerator. "I've got beer, wine, and I made margaritas."

"I'll take a margarita."

"Okay, go get comfy out on the deck, and I'll be right out." He comes to me and kisses me quickly on the lips before opening the door for me.

I sit on the wicker love seat that sits right across from the grill. Since it's light out, I glance around the yard and smile when I see toys in the corner by a shed. Jack comes out carrying a beer and a glass. I take the glass from him. "Thanks." I take a sip and sigh.

"Does it taste okay?"

"It tastes great, thank you."

While he grills, I sip my drink as he tells me about growing up in Wisconsin and that he used to play sports. "I'm not surprised you were a jock. What did you play?"

"Soccer, baseball, basketball—you name it, I played it at some point. Baseball was the sport I was best at. What about you?"

I knew he'd ask. "No sports. I was more of a bookworm. Plus I wasn't very athletic—even now I just stick to yoga or walking because I only run if someone is chasing me." *God, did I just say that?*

"Hmmm...that could be fun." He gives me a grin that makes my belly tighten.

I take a huge drink of my margarita. I need to be careful though because I'm a lightweight, and I don't want to get drunk and make a fool of myself.

We lapse into a comfortable silence, and after he flips the steaks, he shuts the lid and sits down next to me. "Do you sit out here a lot?" I ask.

He rests his arm on the back of our seat. "Not as often as I'd like. Mostly I'm out here when the kids are here. Sometimes when I can't sleep or my hip's bothering me, I come out late at night and swim laps."

"What's wrong with your hip?"

He scrubs a hand over his hair, making it stand up. "You know I'm ex-Special Forces?" I nod. "It was the last time I was deployed. Actually, Reece and I were on a mission together when I got shot. Our team was hit by a sniper, and me and a couple other guys were hit." He looks out across the backyard. "I thought I was dead." Jack doesn't elaborate, but I'm not surprised.

I place my hand on his. "I ended up with a hip replacement," he continues, shaking his head. "Anyway, that's that story. Will you go check the potatoes while I check the steaks and asparagus?"

"Sure." I stand up and head inside to peek in the oven. The potatoes are done, so I grab the potholder and pull them out just as Jack comes in with the steaks and asparagus.

He's quiet while he washes his hands in the sink, and I wish I hadn't asked him about his hip. I can't even imagine what they saw when they were deployed. I'm sure it does a lot to someone to stare death in the eye. I can guarantee his thoughts at the time were all about Delilah and not wanting to leave her.

I stand next to the stove and feel completely unsure of what to do or say. Should I act normal, or my version of normal? Should I apologize?

Luckily I don't have to think too long, because he comes over to me with two plates filled with steak and asparagus. I grab the spatula and scoop one potato up and place it on his plate and then put one on mine. "Do you want to sit outside?" he asks, picking up both of our plates.

"Yeah, that'd be great. Do you want another beer?" Jack nods so I grab him a fresh one and carry it outside to the table he's got outside. He sets our plates down and grabs my drink, sitting it in front of my plate.

Always the gentleman, he pulls out my chair for me. I give him a smile and sit down. My stomach chooses that moment to growl. The food looks delicious, and I lean down to inhale the delicious scent.

As he sits down, he picks up his phone and then music starts playing from somewhere. I look around and he laughs. "Hidden speakers."

"Ahhh...gotcha." I recognize the beginning chords of "Everlong." "Foo Fighters, nice."

I cut into my steak and moan as soon as it hits my tongue. There's a light coating of salt and pepper on it. I look up and Jack's staring at me. "I'm sorry, it's just so good."

Jack smiles before cutting into his own. I clean my plate, savoring every morsel. He gets me another drink after clearing our plates. When he sits back down, I thank him for dinner. "Everything was so delicious."

"I'm glad you liked it." He reaches out, grabbing my hand. "Did you bring your suit?"

I nod, because suddenly it's *extremely* hot out here.

"Good." He takes a pull from his beer, and I can't stop myself from staring at him. The thought of seeing him in nothing but swim trunks makes me so hot that I can't stand it. I grab my drink, draining it with a quickness. "Come on, I'll show you where you can change."

I grab his offered hand and follow him inside. He leads me upstairs and into his bedroom. "I'll grab my trunks and change in the hall bathroom." Jack grabs his trunks out of his dresser and disappears out into the hall.

I dig the extremely tiny bikini out of my bag and quickly change into it. I step into his en suite and look at myself in the mirror. This suit is black with red cherries all over it, and it accentuates my curves but makes them look better.

I step back into his bedroom and feel the butterflies take flight in my belly. I take a deep breath and open the door, stepping out into the hall.

Chapter Eight

Jack

I step out into the hall as soon as I hear my bedroom door open, and I almost swallow my tongue. Harley is wearing the tiniest bikini I've ever seen. I thought she was gorgeous before, but now, she's a fucking knockout. I realize I'm staring and shake myself out of my lust-filled stupor.

"You look incredible," I tell her, but Harley's eyes aren't even on me—they're directed at the crotch of my swim trunks. Can she see I'm half-hard?

"Ummm...what?" Her cheeks turn red as she looks up at my face.

I smile. "I just said you look incredible."

"Thank you. You look great too."

I grab a couple of towels and then Harley's hand, leading her downstairs. I let go of Harley's hand once we reach the kitchen, and grab us a couple of bottles of water. She walks ahead of me, and my eyes go to her luscious heart-shaped ass.

I throw on the lights around—and in—the pool. The music's still playing, but it's soft enough not to bother my neighbors. Harley walks around the pool to the stairs. I watch her walk down until she's submerged up to her waist. "The water feels great. Are you getting in?"

I come around and step down into the pool. I push off the stairs and swim toward her. I stand up, right in front of her. I lean down, kissing her lips slowly and thoroughly.

I move us through the water until it's up to my biceps. I grab her thighs and lift her until her legs are wrapped around my hips. "I could kiss you forever," I whisper against her lips.

"So don't stop," she whispers back.

Harley's arms wind around my shoulders as we begin kissing again. Her unique flavor explodes on my tongue as ours duel. I should be taking this slow, but I can't seem to stop myself. She's making me lose all of my self-control.

I know she can feel that my dick is hard because when she rocks against me, she moans into my mouth. I move us until her back is against the side of the pool. I hold her ass cheek in one hand while the other is braced against the pool wall, caging her in.

I rock against her and already feel the desire to come. Of course it's been a couple of years since I've had sex. *Fuck,* I should've jerked off before she got here. Even through my swim trunks and her bottoms, I can feel the heat of her pussy.

I let go of the side of the pool and reach between us. Harley moans as I begin rubbing her clit. She writhes in my embrace, her arms tightening around my shoulders. Fuck, she's going to come right here in my arms.

One of her arms disappears from around my shoulders, and through my swim trunks she starts stroking my cock. A groan slips from my mouth. Suddenly Harley stiffens, her eyes squeeze shut, and a whimper escapes her lips. Just the sight of her coming has me following suit, like I'm in high school again and can't control myself.

She pulls her lips away from mine but leans in until her forehead is resting against my own. I watch the rapid rise and fall of her chest. Harley cups my face in her hands and I look into her eyes. Something important passes between the two of us, and as much as it fucking scares me, it also excites me.

"That was awesome," Harley says.

I can't help myself—I throw my head back and laugh. God, it feels good to *really* laugh. I get control of myself and nod. "Yeah, and I feel like a teenager again, coming quicker then I wanted to."

We stay in the pool for a little while longer before I'm leading her out. I wrap my towel around my waist and grab hers to dry her off inch by inch. I lay her towel down on the lounger and pull her with me until we're lying on it.

I'm on top of her, and her legs are wrapped around me again. The seal has been broken and I can't get enough of her. I know the moment I taste her pussy I'll be lost, because I'm already addicted to her.

My hand glides up her side until I reach her

bikini-covered breasts. I stroke my thumb over her nipple, feeling it harden. I give it a little pinch—she arches her back and moans. My lips leave hers.

"Jack, what about your neighbors?" Harley whispers.

I push up on my forearms and look down at her. "The neighbors on the left are on vacation, and the house on the right is vacant. The fence along the back is high enough no one can see. Don't worry—I won't let anyone see you."

She smiles, giving me a view of her pearly whites. "Okay."

My dick is hard again and I have a feeling it's always going to be that way when I'm with her. I rock my hips, letting her feel what she does to me. Harley gasps when I make contact with her clit.

I can't take it; I need to taste her. I get off the lounger and then scoop her up, throwing her over my shoulder. "Umm…Jack, what are you doing?" she squeals.

I slap her ass. "Hush."

"Don't you tell me what to do," she says with a huff that makes me laugh.

Once inside the house, I dump her on the ottoman that Delilah *said* I needed. I get down on my knees and watch her chest move up and down as she watches me pull her bikini bottoms down. I look down and a groan slips past my lips as I stare at her bare pussy. "Did you do this for me?"

Harley bites her lower lip and nods.

"Mmmm…thank you, baby."

I grab the backs of her thighs and push them back. I lean in and drag my tongue from the opening of her pussy up to her clit. Her flavor explodes on my tongue. Harley's fingers grip my hair as my control snaps, and I attack her pussy with vigor.

Her cries and the way she jerks her hips tell me she loves what I'm doing. I stiffen my tongue, then thrust it inside her tight channel. She moans as I begin to fuck her. She's so close to coming, and she's so wet her arousal is all over my chin, but I don't care. I pull back before pushing one finger inside her.

Harley begins grinding against my hand, and it's so fucking sexy. "Undo your top." I barely recognize my own voice. I watch as she reaches behind her neck and then slowly pulls the top down until her breasts are exposed.

Her pink nipples harden immediately and I lean over her—she still has a grip on my hair, and it tightens as I suck one nipple into my mouth. Harley lets out a surprised cry as she begins coming. *Fuck,* she's squeezing my finger, and I can only imagine how good it'll feel when she squeezes my cock.

I ease her down slowly from her orgasm and release her nipple with a *pop*. I pull my finger out of her and suck it into my mouth. She tastes tangy and sweet, and once my finger is clean I lean up and she pulls me to her mouth.

Our kiss is hungry, intense, and my cock is aching—begging to be inside her. I break our kiss. "Hold onto me." She wraps her arms around my shoulders and her legs around my waist.

With ease I stand up with her wrapped around me and carry her up the stairs, tossing her onto my big-ass bed. I love the way her tits jiggle as she bounces on the mattress, but what I love best is the sound of her laughter.

Even before Becky became the bitch that she was, she never laughed...she never joked around. All we seemed to do was fuck and fight, and toward the end it was more of the latter. "Stay right here. I'll be right back."

I head into my bathroom, grab a wet washcloth, and quickly wipe myself off from when I came in my swim trunks. My dick is so hard right now, I decide to just strip out of them, turn off the bathroom light, and step back into my bedroom. Harley's eyes stay on me as I crawl onto the bed.

She pushes up and holds out her hand to stop me. "Lie on your back?" I raise my brow. Harley looks down at my cock, and I swear she licks her fucking lips. My dick loves it, and jerks. "I-I want to taste you." I flip onto my back, and Harley wastes no time climbing on top of me.

She sits on my stomach and looks down at me. "I'm not usually so forward." Harley bends down until we're chest to chest. "You're such a beautiful man, Jack." Her thumb strokes back and forth across my lower lip.

I don't even know what to say. It's the sweetest fucking thing someone's ever said to me. I pull her to me, kissing her lips harder than I intended to, but she just moans and sinks into it. Harley pulls away first and begins kissing her way down my body.

I groan as she sucks and nips at my nipple, and then she moves to the other. She shimmies down my body, kissing and licking a path straight to my cock. When Harley reaches the scars on my hip, she kisses each and every one of the pale lines. The scars are ugly, but then again the bullet did a lot of damage.

Shit, I was told I'd walk with a limp for the rest of my life, but I powered through painful rehab and have kept myself strong and fit. Now I'm in better shape than when I was in my early thirties.

I groan as she continues to trace my scar and wraps her free hand around my dick, pumping it slowly. When she's done kissing my scar, she holds my dick so it stands straight up and leans forward, wasting no time swallowing my cock down.

"Oh fuck, baby," I moan.

Her hair is half in and half out of the knot on top of her head, and I grab it in my fists. Her head bobs up and down and I swear I'm going to come really, *really* soon. "Fuck, you know how to suck cock." Her moans vibrate around my shaft. "Baby, I'm gonna come so fucking hard."

Harley increases her efforts, and in an embarrassingly short amount of time I feel the tingle at the base of my spine. "Pull back unless you're going to swallow me down."

I swear she sucks harder, and I thrust up as I begin to shoot my cum down her throat. I feel it as she swallows me down and groans.

As soon as my softening cock slips from her mouth, I pull her up and on top of me. I kiss her lips, not even giving a shit that I just came in her mouth. I roll us until we're both on our sides and chest to chest. Neither of us says anything, and I watch her watching her fingers trace the tattoo on my chest; it's a Celtic knot that means father and daughter.

"I'm glad you came over tonight," I tell her quietly.

Harley kisses my chest and whispers back, "I am too."

"How about this…we get dressed—and by that I mean you in panties and one of my t-shirts—and then we go downstairs and have dessert." I hate to say after coming twice I'm going to need a little bit of time to recover.

"Mmmm…some dessert sounds good."

I climb out of bed and slip on a pair of basketball shorts. Off the chair in the corner I grab her the t-shirt I was wearing earlier. I don't know what it is, but the thought of her in my shirt gets me hard—well, semi-hard for right now. "Come here, baby." Harley climbs off the bed and walks toward me. "Lift your arms."

She does what I ask and I slip it over her head. It hits her mid-thigh and looks sexy as fuck. I grab her hand and drag her downstairs with me. I have her sit at the breakfast bar while I pull the brownies Delilah made out of the refrigerator.

After cutting a couple of pieces and placing them in bowls, I stick them in the microwave. While they heat up, I grab the vanilla ice cream out of the freezer. I scoop ice cream onto the brownies and pour chocolate sauce on top.

I bring them around and sit next to Harley. "Oh my God, that looks amazing."

"You can thank Del for this. She thought you might like something sweet." My daughter, Miss

Matchmaker...the minute she figured out that I was into Harley, she became my biggest cheerleader.

I know Becky did a number on both of us, and because of that I've shied away from relationships or real intimacy. The older Del got the more worried I was that she'd have issues—granted, after Charlie's birth she struggled, but that stemmed more from the events that occurred prior to my little nugget's birth.

I'm still not sure I'm "relationship material," but I want to try—at least with Harley I do. A moan from her has me turning and watching her bite into a huge wad of ice cream and brownie. Now....my dick's hard again.

"What?" she says with her mouth full.

I lean forward, licking the drizzle of chocolate syrup off of her lips. I pull back and see that Harley's eyes are glazed over. "You had some chocolate on your lip."

"Oh...you do too," she says right before her chocolate-covered finger paints my lips. Before I can say anything, Harley is licking the syrup off. She leans back and smiles at me.

I raise my brow. "Did you get it all?"

She shrugs. "Maybe." Harley goes back to eating her dessert, and I dig into mine.

When we finish our ice cream, I make us some coffee and we snuggle up in the family room. We drink our coffee and put in *Remember the Titans*. Once we finish our coffee, I lie with my back against the cushions and Harley tucked into my front.

By the time the movie is over, she's out like a

light. I carefully climb off the sectional and then scoop her up into my arms. She doesn't even budge as I carry her upstairs. I gently lay her down, and then head into the bathroom. I freeze because I have a dried chocolate ring around my lips.

I shake my head and smile. This woman is doing crazy things to me already. I can only imagine what it's going to be like if this goes how I want it to. I can only hope that I don't fuck it up—because there is a possibility that could happen.

With that thought, I crawl into bed with her, pull her into my arms, and immediately fall asleep.

Chapter Nine

Harley

I open my eyes and sigh. *That sun is sure bright today*, I think as I roll over and burrow further into the covers. My eyes pop open because I realize I'm not in my bed—I'm in Jack's. Last night had been one of the best dates in my whole life. I still can't believe that we did all that naughty stuff last night.

I wouldn't say that I'm very experienced sexually, but the oral he gave me last night was the best I've ever had. Guys like Jack probably have lots of lady friends, and I hope when I gave him a blowjob I didn't embarrass myself. He's got the biggest dick I've ever seen, and definitely bigger than the other guys I was with.

I'm shocked that Jack didn't fuck me with it last night…I wanted him to—*God*, I wanted him to. After his blowjob I swore he was going to want to be inside me, but instead we went downstairs, ate dessert, and then snuggled on his huge sectional. I hate that I fell asleep, but snuggling up to him after a couple of awesome orgasms and chocolate made it easy for me to pass out.

I climb out of Jack's bed and grab my brush, face wash, and toothbrush. In his bathroom I take care of business and, still dressed in his t-shirt, I head downstairs. The scent of bacon hits me as soon as I reach the bottom of the stairs.

A rock song can be heard as soon as I step into the kitchen. Jack's got his back to me and I take in the beauty that is his body. His shoulders are broad, and my eyes travel down to his narrow waist. His basketball shorts hang low on hips.

Jack turns as I step farther into the room. "Morning, baby." *Ohh*...I like that. "Come here." I take his offered hand and let him pull me into a hug. I lift my lips to him and expect just a quick peck, but instead he kisses me deeply. Our tongues lightly duel before he pulls away. "How did you sleep?"

"I slept really, *really* well. I'm sorry I fell asleep on you last night." Jack pours me a cup of coffee and grabs the creamer for me. I pour a healthy dose into my cup and then lean against the counter, taking a sip.

"That's okay. I only stayed up until the movie was over. Oh, and thanks for not telling me I still had a ring of chocolate around my lips." He shakes his head.

I, of course, burst into laughter.

"Oh, you think it's funny?" I nod, and he grabs me around the waist. I squeal and try to get away from him, but his grip is strong.

Jack bites me where my neck and shoulder meet, and I do a full body shudder. He kisses me, and then releases me. "What can I do to help?" I ask.

"If you want to crack some eggs and get them ready for scrambling, that'd be great." I do as he asks and grab the carton.

Once that's all done, we sit together at the breakfast bar and dig in. "This is delicious, thank you."

"You're welcome."

We're quiet while we both eat, and when we finish I start cleaning up, but he stops me. I turn to him. "What are your plans for the day?" Oh God, did that sound too needy, or like I expect him to spend the day with me?

"Workout, and then I thought about offering to babysit so Delilah and Reece could have a night out." He grabs my hand and pulls me to him. "What about you?"

"I need to write for a little bit and do some other stuff, and that's it."

"Well, why don't you come over tonight while I'm babysitting and we'll order pizza, unless that doesn't sound appealing to you."

"That sounds really good, actually." Not wanting to wear out my welcome, I say, "I think I'm going to head home so I can get some writing done." I head upstairs and change into my clothes I brought to wear home. I stuff my outfit from the day before into my bag.

I throw it over my shoulder and Jack meets me at the bottom of the stairs. "I had a really good time last night." That makes me extremely happy, but I conceal it the best I can. As much as I like Jack, he's got "heartbreak" written all over him. It'd be best if I kept somewhat of a distance from him, but I'll do that tomorrow.

"I did too, Jack. Thank you for having me." He walks me to the door and we share one more intense kiss before I walk in a euphoric daze to my car.

"I'll text you when I plan on being next door."

I turn. "My bed isn't as big as yours, but you're welcome to stay tonight."

Jack gives me a smile and nods. "Okay."

He watches me from the door and gives me a hand flick as I pull away.

All the way home I smile, and I know that I'm in big, *big* trouble with that man. But I just can't drum up enough of a reason to care.

***

My fingers fly over the keyboard as I work on finishing this chapter of my newest book. I wasn't sure where this story was going, but when I got home and sat down, the words just began to flow. I finish the chapter I'm working on and save the document.

I stand up and do some stretches. My body always gets stiff after a major marathon writing session. I head into the kitchen and pour myself a glass of iced tea and grab a banana. Back in my office, I pull up my emails and shoot a quick one to my editor, letting her know that I'm on schedule.

I go through the rest of my emails and I see a familiar name. I swear I feel my blood pressure rise. I almost just want to delete it, but morbid curiosity has me pull it up.

> *Ms. Steele,*
> *I hope you received my gift. If you threw them in the trash, then that's exactly where they belong. Don't forget God will punish you, and if you're not careful, so will I.*
> *Colossians 3:25: For the wrongdoer will be paid back for the wrong he has done, and there is no partiality.*
> *Yours in Jesus,*
> *Martha*

I move the cursor over the reply button. I know I shouldn't click on it, and that's what everyone has told me, but this is bordering on threatening and has me kind of spooked. I decide not to because I know that I could piss this person off even more, and they already seem plenty pissed at me.

Maybe I should print it out so Jack can look at it. I know he wanted me to tell him if I got emailed again, but I don't want to burden him with this. Ugh…what to do, what to do?

I decide to save it for now, and maybe I'll talk to him later. I save the email in a folder I mark,

"Stuff for Jack."

I make my way into the kitchen and whip up a quick sandwich. I lean against the counter while I eat. Once I finish, I grab Fifty out of his cage and lay out some greens for him. While he munches on it, I clean out his cage and give him fresh food and water.

Once that's done I put his leash on him and take him outside to hop around the yard. I wrap his leash around my wrist so he doesn't jump away and he's not far from me while I pull weeds in my flower beds.

"Hey, Harley." I turn and see Delilah standing at the entrance to the backyard.

I stand up and wipe my hands off on my shorts. I bend down and pick Fifty up in my arms. I've never seen someone who has that beautiful pregnancy glow, but she's radiant. I've never seen her mom, but I've seen Jack so it's no surprise that she's gorgeous. It's almost a little intimidating.

"Hi, Del. How are you?" Every time I see her, her little baby bump gets bigger and bigger. "You look great."

She strokes a hand over her belly. "Thanks. I swear I'm bigger than with either of the other kids. Of course I wasn't planning on this one, but we love surprises in this family." Delilah picks up Fifty out of my hands, snuggling him to her chest. "My dad's watching the kids for us tonight. He says that you're coming over to help."

My face heats up and I look anywhere but at Delilah. I turn back to her when she places her hand on my arm. "I'm sorry, I'm not trying to make you uncomfortable. I shouldn't have said anything." She says the last bit softly, almost to herself.

"It's seriously okay. You didn't...I'm just worried because what if things don't work out? I'd hate to lose you as a friend. To be honest I don't have many friends, and I don't want to lose that."

I hate admitting that, but there's no sense in

lying about it. For as long as I've known Delilah and Reece I haven't had people over, and I hang out with them and their friends.

"I promise you that no matter what happens with him, you will *always* be my friend." She sets Fifty down and wraps her arms around me. "I mean it, okay?"

I nod. "Thank you for that."

We talk for a few more minutes before she walks back over to her house. I pick up Fifty, carry him inside, and put him in his cage. In my bedroom, I pull out some clean clothes and take a shower.

After I'm finished I throw on my black jogging shorts and an old Britney Spears t-shirt. I decide to go makeup free and blow dry my hair before putting it in a high ponytail.

I head into the living room and peek out the front window; I see Jack's truck, but instead of it being in Reece and Del's driveway, it's in mine.

There's something about seeing his truck parked in my driveway, but I push it away. I have to remind myself that eventually everyone leaves me. *Ugh, how could I let myself forget that?* I was blinded by a few really amazing orgasms.

I flop down on the couch and sigh. Now I want to just sit here and pout, but I don't—instead I stand up and shake off the melancholy. In the kitchen I pour myself half a glass of wine, but pour it back into the bottle.

I grab a Coke Zero out of the refrigerator, grab my keys, and then head next door.

***

I close the book in my hand and smile down at the sleeping princess snuggled up next to me. Tonight has been such a good night, and my pity party ended immediately. Charlie immediately had me build her a fort that we sat in while we watched Disney movie after Disney movie.

Poor little Jackson tried getting in it with us, but Charlie would shout, "No boys" and chase him out. She finally let him in when Jack crawled in with him. After the fort and movies, we had pizza together.

For a brief moment I could picture in my head that this could be Jack and I with our children. Yes, I know that's jumping the gun, but a girl can dream, can't she? After we ate, I washed both kids up while Jack straightened the kitchen.

Both the kids had baths before I got there, so I helped Jack get them into their jammies. I think Jack even made me fall in love with him a little bit; he was so good with his grandkids. They climbed all over him, and he didn't even care.

It was very obvious that they both love him very much, especially Charlie, but then again, I can understand the bond they share since Jack is the one who delivered her.

When Jack gave little Jackson his last bottle and rocked him asleep it made my heart swell, but then it also made me sad. If I ever get lucky and have children, they would only have *his parents* to be grandparents.

Now I'm lying on a *Frozen* comforter with Charlie snuggled against me. I ease off the bed and then cover her with her blanket. I bend down, brushing one of her wild brunette curls away from her little cherub face and kiss her forehead.

When I stand up, I freeze. Jack's watching me from the doorway with a look on his face that warms me all over. On my way out of her room, I turn on her nightlight. I reach Jack and he pulls me into his arms. He doesn't say anything—just continues to stare at me.

"W-What, Jack?"

He says nothing but then he just bends down and takes my lips in a fierce kiss. Somehow he gets us downstairs and then I'm straddling him on the couch. Jack grips my ponytail, holding me immobile.

I grind against his cock, which is rock hard. Jack moans into my mouth, and I swear I get extremely wet. I grip his t-shirt in my fist, and I'm so blind with lust right now.

"Oh shit!"

I fly up off the couch with Jack standing behind me as Reece and Delilah walk into the living room. My face, I'm sure, is a dark shade of red right now. "I-uh...I-uh...Hi."

I try to step away from Jack, but he rests his hands on my shoulders and whispers in my ear, "Don't move."

I'm not stupid—I know he's using me to hide that fact that he has an erection from his daughter. Delilah can't stop smiling, and Reece is coughing to—very poorly—disguise his laughter.

I swear I could seriously cry right now—I'm completely mortified. Maybe Del can tell because she very casually asks how the kids were.

"They were great. Jackson went to bed real good, but Charlie tried to squeeze out as many bedtime stories as she could get before she finally passed out," Jack says, and his erection is obviously gone because he moves around me to pick up the fort blankets from the floor.

"I appreciate you guys watching them," Reece says as he moves to help Jack with the mess on the floor.

Delilah asks me to join her in the kitchen for some tea. Once there, she gets the water going and then sits across from me. "What did you guys end up doing?" I ask.

"We went for dinner and then went to see the new Keanu Reeves movie." She places her hands over her heart. "He gets better and better with age."

I nod in agreement. It's obvious she's trying to make me—*again*—feel at ease. The tea kettle whistles, and Del gets up. I watch her as she pours each of us a cup. "What do you take in your tea?"

"Um...milk and sugar, please." She returns to the table with both of our cups. Del takes a sip and sighs. "I miss coffee, but I've figured out how to make this almost as good...*almost*."

I take a sip, and I'm not a huge fan of tea, but this is pretty good. The guys join us, and I feel just a little awkward when Jack sits next to me and puts his arm on the back of my chair, leaning into me.

We don't hang out long before Del starts yawning, and to be honest I'm tired too. I stand up with Jack following. They walk us to the door, and Del gives me a hug. Reece surprises me by doing the same.

Jack leads me outside, grabs my hand in his, and walks me to my house. I grab my keys and unlock the door. It's not even a second thought to bring Jack inside. I lock the front door and drop my keys on the kitchen counter.

I feel him behind me and do a full body shiver as he brushes my ponytail away from my neck. His lips move slowly up my neck, causing goosebumps to break out all over my skin. Jack nips my earlobe and I moan.

He grips my ponytail, using it to tip my head back. I think he's going to kiss my lips, but instead he begins to lick and nip the skin at the base of my throat. I whimper and hold onto the counter to keep myself from falling over.

With his free hand, Jack reaches around and cups my breast, tweaking my nipple through my bra. I moan and writhe as he assaults every inch of my neck. It's quite possible that I could have an orgasm right now.

Jack pulls away and roughly turns me around. I'm suddenly in his arms with my legs wrapped around his waist. I grab his face and slam my lips down on his. He moves through my house and then crawls onto my bed with me still wrapped around him.

He wastes no time getting me naked—it's like I've suddenly unleashed the beast inside him. I swear a growl rips from his throat as he moves down my body, sucking one nipple into his mouth. Jack nips the tip, causing me to cry out and arch my back.

He gives the other nipple the same treatment.

Again he begins to descend down my body until he reaches my pussy. Jack wastes no time dragging his tongue through my wet folds and sucking my clit into his mouth.

This man eats pussy like he's on a mission. I moan as he pushes one, then two fingers inside me. He tickles that ridge inside me that makes my body shudder so violently that he has to pin my hips down with an arm across them.

Jack sucks my clit into his mouth, tickles that spot, and then presses down on my lower stomach. A pressure builds and I try pushing his head away, or pulling it closer—I'm so dizzy I can't tell which is happening.

When I come, I come so hard my vision goes white. I know I'm gushing all over Jack and I can't even think...I can't even drum up enough brainpower to be embarrassed.

I'm barely aware of what's happening before I feel Jack thrust inside me. He kisses me and I taste myself, and fuck me, I'm ready to come again. Jack pulls almost all the way out before thrusting back in. He groans against my mouth, and it makes me quiver.

I feel so full, and even though I'm very wet, it's still a tight fit. "Fuck baby, you feel so good," Jack says against my lips before pulling almost all the way out and slamming back into me. "Shit, I'm close already." He reaches between us and begins to strum my clit.

The feeling below starts to build. Jack grabs my thigh, pulling it up and increasing his thrusts. I cry out as he hits me so deep inside there's a bite of pain, but I welcome it. "Jack," I moan as I begin to come again.

If it's even possible, he starts thrusting harder until he plants himself, buries his face in my neck, and groans as I feel him begin to come.

I stroke his back as we both struggle to catch our breath. Jack pushes up and smiles down at me. "Are you okay? I think I lost control a little bit there."

I'm smiling like a loon, but I don't care. I reach up, stroking his cheek. "I'm great."

"Good. Let me get rid of this condom." Oh God, I didn't even realize that he'd put one on. He eases out of me and kisses me between my breasts before disappearing out into the hall, and then a few minutes later he returns to my room.

God, he is so sexy. That's all I can think as he walks back into the bedroom in all his naked glory. He crawls into bed beside me and pulls me into his arms. "I'm on the wet spot," I say, snuggling into him. "But I don't care."

He flips us around, and I snuggle back into him. "Thank you for spending time with me and the kids tonight."

"You're welcome. I had a lot of fun."

Jack kisses my forehead, and I feel myself falling asleep. The last thought I have is that I'm in trouble. I'm falling for this man already, but I don't think I could stop it if I tried.

Chapter Ten

Harley

I roll over in bed and moan. My body aches, but it was so worth it. I know it'd been a long time since I've been with someone and the same for him—of course he knew how to play my body, causing me to come multiple times.

I reach out and touch his side of the bed and it's cold. Did he leave? I sniff the air and don't smell food cooking. After climbing out of bed, I throw on a pair of sweatpants and a tank top, go into the bathroom and take care of business, then wash my face and brush my teeth.

"Jack?" I call out, but he doesn't answer. In the living room I peek out the window and see that his truck is still in the driveway. I move to let Fifty out of his cage, but the door is open and he's not in there.

In the kitchen I find a pot of coffee and pour myself a cup. I move toward the back door and look out. My heart—I swear—skips a beat as I take in the sight in front of me. Jack is in the backyard with Fifty on his leash and Charlie next to him with her little hand in his.

The way he's smiling at her is a thing of pure beauty. I reach up and touch the tears that are leaking from my eyes. I hate myself because I'm jealous. I hope that sweet little girl knows how lucky she is to have so many people who love her.

I hurry down the hall to my bathroom and splash some cold water on my face. I take a deep breath and get myself together. When I step out into the hall, I hear the back door open.

"Whewes Hawey?" I hear as I walk down the hall.

"She's sleeping, sweetheart," Jack answers her.

Moving into the kitchen, I smile when Charlie sees me. "Hi, sweetheart." She charges me, and I pick her up. "What are you doing?"

"Papa and Fiffy was outside. I go see them." She wraps her arms around my neck. "I'm hungwy."

"How about some pancakes?" I ask her and then look at Jack. "Do pancakes sound okay?"

"I actually need to get going. I've got a case I'm working on and need to do some follow-up."

Okay, I wasn't expecting that. I watch him put Fifty back in his cage and lay his leash on top.

I set Charlie down and she goes over to Jack and takes his hand. "I'm going to take her home, and then head out." He comes to me and kisses me quickly on the lips. "I'll call you later."

Just like that he's gone, and I feel like I was just given the kiss of death. I lock the back door and pour myself a cup of coffee. After popping a piece of toast in the toaster, I slather it in almond butter and then carry it back into my office. Drowning myself in work will be the perfect way for me to distract myself from wondering about Jack and his sudden departure.

I slip on my noise-canceling headphones, pull up my book, and turn on Pandora.

After two solid hours of watching the blinking cursor, I stand up from my desk. My body is stiff and sore and I take some ibuprofen. I decide to take a break because I just can't focus, and there's no sense in sitting in front of my computer when the words aren't coming.

I remember when writer's block used to happen in the beginning and I would freak out and cry. Now, I just take a break and try to relax and clear my mind.

In my bedroom I close the room-darkening shades and crawl onto my bed. I bury my nose in the pillow that Jack slept on and inhale his unique woodsy scent. I curl up and clear my mind, and in no time I feel myself fade into a deep sleep.

Bam, bam, bam...Bam, bam, bam.

I push up in my bed. "What's going on?" I murmur, my voice gruff with sleep.

Stumbling out of bed, I make my way down the hall and look out the window. Jack is at the door fiddling with the lock. I quickly unlock the door and pull it open. Jack rushes in, wrapping his arms around me. "*Thank God.* You didn't answer your phone. Del came over and knocked and knocked, and you didn't answer."

"I-I was having some writer's block and laid

down for a bit." That's when I notice it's dusk. "What time is it?"

He kisses my forehead and pulls back. "It's seven."

"Oh geez, I slept all day." My stomach growls loudly and Jack chuckles.

"Do you want me to order a pizza?"

I'm so confused right now, and I seriously thought when he left he was gone for good. "Um...yeah, pizza sounds great. I'm going to go get freshened up." Jack pulls out his phone and kisses me before disappearing into my kitchen.

In the bathroom I brush my teeth and my hair before braiding it. When I head back into the kitchen Jack's on the phone but holds his hand out to me. "Yeah, sweetheart, she was just asleep and didn't hear us." He listens, and I can hear Delilah's voice but not what she's saying. "I love you too."

He sets his phone down and wraps his arms around me. "Sorry I worried you guys. I took some ibuprofen and maybe it knocked me out."

"I'm just glad you're okay. I ordered us a large pizza with the works. Is that okay?"

I nod and grab the pitcher of iced tea out of the refrigerator, pouring us both a glass.

When the pizza comes we sit on the couch and demolish half of it. We finish eating and I take the leftover pizza into the kitchen and shove it into the refrigerator. I grab Jack a beer and join him back on the couch.

You'd think because I slept all day I'd be wide awake, but instead I rest my head on Jack's shoulder while we finish up some western with

Chris Pratt and Denzel Washington in it. It isn't longer before I'm in snoozeville.

I wake as I'm being lifted, and snuggle into him. "I'm sorry I fell asleep. This guy wore me out last night and maybe he zapped all of my energy."

"Oh yeah? I bet he was really good-looking."

I giggle and bury my face in his neck, but then pull out. "Ehh...he was okay."

In my room he tosses me on the bed and follows me down. "Just *okay*?" He begins tickling my sides until I'm squealing and screaming.

"Okay, *stop*! You're hot!" Jack does and then he moves us around until I'm situated lying partially on top of him.

We snuggle up together on my bed, and I draw imaginary circles on his stomach. "Did you get your work done earlier?"

"Yeah, I just had some follow-up phone calls to make, but I got them done."

I burrow closer. "What made you decide to open Rogue?"

"Before I was discharged from the Army, I knew I wanted to do something that I could use my skills at. I actually worked for another company first, but the guy didn't know what the fuck he was doing. Egan and I actually worked together there, and we got to be friends. I brought up the idea for Rogue and he told me if I did it that he'd come work for me."

He gives me a squeeze. "Right before I quit, I started looking into getting the paperwork I needed. To make an extremely dull, long story short, I leased the office space, hired Egan, and then Erik—

the rest is history."

"It sounds like you guys do an amazing job. Did you ever find out if they could pick up any prints on the box?"

Jack sighs. "Unfortunately too many people handled it. They couldn't get a clear print. My buddy said the P.O. Box was a dummy address so they couldn't trace it to anyone. Basically it was a dead end. Have you gotten any more emails?"

I hesitate, but I know I need to tell him. "Yeah, she asked me if I liked the gift she sent and if I threw it in the trash, because that's where it belongs."

He climbs out of my bed and pulls me up with him. He stalks down the hall to my office, flips on the light, and stands next to my computer. "Pull up the email."

I sit down at my desk and do as he says. I get up and he sits down. "What are you doing?"

"I'm forwarding this to Egan to see if he can trace it and find the origin of the email. I wish you still had the others."

I'm starting to see that deleting them wasn't the smartest move. "I wish I still had them too. At the time I just didn't think they were important."

Jack pulls me down onto his lap. "Not important? You don't know how fucked up people are. If this person is targeting you, it could get really nasty. Hopefully Egan will be able to find the origin."

"I wasn't freaked out before, but I am now."

He stands up, sets me down on my feet, and pulls me into his arms. "Don't be freaked, but it wouldn't hurt to keep the doors locked even during the day. If you want, we can get some security cameras set up."

I shake my head. "I don't think I need all of that."

"Well, I want you to tell me right away if you receive any emails, any more packages. I don't care. Even if you think that something is insignificant, I want you to tell me." I hate to admit that he's kind of sexy when he's all growly and bossy.

"I promise I'll tell you." I wrap my arms tightly around his waist. "Why do people have to be so mean? I write erotic romance, but the main component is love. What's so wrong with that? Doesn't everyone want love?"

Jack's body stiffens and I know I've said too much, or he thinks that's what I want from him. Oh sure I do, but I'm going to deny it because in reality love only exists for a lucky few, and I'm just not one of them.

I let go of him and back up. He moves toward me. "This is going to sound terrible, and I don't want it to, but I'm not relationship material. The shit with Del's mom fucked me up."

Is it possible to fall in love with someone in a very short period of time? Is it possible that I've made a mistake falling for the man in front of me? I shouldn't have done it because he treated me so hot and cold before, but I still gave him a chance.

"You know, I'm really tired. I think I'm going to head to bed. Lock up on your way out."

I feel him step up behind me. "I should've stayed away from you."

"I never said I was looking for love. What I meant was everyone loves to read about falling in love." I motion between us. "This just started between us, but thanks for doing me the favor and ending this now before I became too invested in someone who isn't 'relationship material.'"

"We'll talk tomorrow," he says, moving toward the front door.

"I don't think so. I think you and I have said all that we need to." Jack stares at me, and I don't let him see the hurt I feel. It shouldn't be there at all because *we*—or whatever *we* were was so new. "Take care, Jack."

I step into my bedroom, shutting the door behind me. I lean against the door and slide down until my butt hits the floor.

When the front door opens and closes about five minutes later, it's then that I let the tears flow.

***

It's been a week since whatever Jack and I had ended. I've drowned myself in work, which luckily, hasn't been affected by my melancholy. As of now I'm ahead of schedule so…thank you, Jack.

Egan, Jack's IT guy, called me to tell me he was looking into the email and would call me if anything came up. I thought about telling him to refer me to someone else, but he's the best. He also asked me to forward any more emails that I get from Martha.

I think Delilah and Reece know something happened—they've been overly friendly. I've seen

Jack's truck at their house a couple of times so I've stayed in the house like a shut-in until he leaves.

Now, I carry Fifty and his leash outside and take him over to my butterfly garden. After I attach his leash, I set him on the ground. I smile as he nibbles on some grass. The butterflies flit around, and I tip my head back, letting the sun warm my skin.

"Fifty, let's go for a walk." I pick him up and walk around the side of the house to the front.

We walk down the sidewalk, and I smile while I watch kids in a yard down the street chase each other.

"Is that a bunny?" I hear a little voice ask.

"Sam, wait for me." A man comes up behind the little boy. He's really handsome: tall, lean, with dark blond hair and deep brown eyes.

"Dad, look at this bunny. It's so cool, can I get one?"

The man holds out his hand to me. "Hi, I'm Tanner. This is Sam."

I don't feel like talking, but I still shake his hand. "I'm Harley, and this is Fifty." Tanner raises his eyebrow. "Yeah, he's named after *those* books."

"Can I pet him?"

I squat down in front of the little boy, who looks like a tiny version of his father. "Sure, just be gentle."

He very carefully strokes Fifty's back. "He's so soft. What kind of bunny is he?"

"He's a Lionhead Lop, and yes, he's very soft. While I work he sleeps on a little bed on my desk. He's the laziest bunny I've *ever* met." He giggles, and it makes me smile.

"Hawey!" I know that voice and turn to see Charlie, Reece, and Jack walking down the sidewalk.

"I better get going, but it was nice meeting you guys." I start walking toward them, but keep my eyes on Charlie; she reaches me first. "Hi, sweetheart." I look at both Reece and Jack, but Jack's gaze is focused on something behind me. I don't care, though—that way I can avoid him. "Hey, Reece."

Reece gives me a smile. "Hey, Harley."

I bend down and hug Charlie and then walk around them, heading back down to my house. As soon as I'm inside I lock the door and put Fifty in his cage. I decide to take myself out for a nice dinner.

I've already showered, so all I need to do is freshen up. I've never had a problem eating alone. Honestly, I usually just catch up on my reading or do some plotting. When you're alone ninety percent of the time anyway, it's very easy to do stuff alone without being self-conscious about it.

I throw on a pair of black skinny capris, a sleeveless red button-up shirt, and my black wedge sandals. In the bathroom I brush out my hair and pin it to the top of my head in a knot. I just brush some powder all over my face and swipe on some lip gloss.

I grab my purse and Kindle and head out to my car. I ignore the fact that Jack is sitting on Del and Reece's front steps, looking beautiful with Jackson on his lap—also ignoring the fact that his eyes are on me. I head to Maggiano's, my favorite, and they seat me in a little booth in the bar.

I push away my plate of ravioli. I'm so full and can't eat another bite. My waitress brings me the check and I give her my card. Once I pay, I grab my purse and head out to the parking lot. With a full belly, I know I'm going to sleep well tonight. I pull out of the parking lot.

I'm not ready to head home yet, so I decide to go for a drive. But first, I stop at Starbucks for a latte. I take a sip and then put my drink in the cup holder. When I glance up at my rearview mirror, I notice the car behind me is following too closely.

I step on the accelerator and get ahead of them, but the person behind me speeds up too. Traffic is light and again I speed up, but so do they. My heart starts to race and I blindly reach for my phone.

I hold onto the steering wheel with one hand and hold my phone up with the other. A jolt causes me to cry out and my phone to fall to the floor.

The car hits me harder this time, and I slide into the intersection. The light turns red, but I can't stop. I don't see the huge truck heading straight at my driver's side until it's too late.

***

Beep...beep...beep. My eyes flutter open. "You're going to be okay, baby." What's Jack doing in my dream? I close my eyes and fade into nothing.

Chapter Eleven

Jack

Earlier when I'd seen Harley talking to that man down the street, I swear I had the urge to mark my territory. I'd lost that right, but I was having a hard time accepting that. Later, when she left all dressed up, I thought maybe she had a date. I wanted to stay at my daughter's until Harley got home, but they booted me out.

My daughter can be firecracker, and she was *not* happy with me. I was on my way home to stew in my own stupidity when I ended up at a major intersection, idling at a stoplight. Right in front of my eyes, I watched a car run the red light before a truck plowed into it—a second car was right behind the one that ran the red light, but it took off in the other direction.

It took me only a moment to recognize the model and license plate of the destroyed car and realize the victim was Harley. I was out of my truck and running toward the car before I could think, only barely noticing someone shouting out that they were calling 9-1-1. The driver's side was completely smashed in, and I had to get to her through the passenger side.

When I placed my fingers at her neck and felt her pulse I was able to relax…a little. I was in the middle of assessing her when the paramedics, firefighters, and police showed up. They had to use the Jaws of Life to get her out of her car, and the moment they had her on the stretcher, I asked them where they were taking her.

I hopped in my truck and followed them to the ER. I knew they had the driver that hit her in the other ambulance, and luckily he seemed to be okay. It was more of a precaution.

In the emergency room they wouldn't let me see her at first. They had to run numerous tests on her before they'd let me back. Delilah came and sat with me while we waited to hear what was going on. Of course I didn't actually sit—I paced back and forth.

Guilt plagued me because Harley had scared me when she started talking about love. And what did I do instead of just fucking telling her? I ran because I'm a dumbass, stupid motherfucker, and my daughter and son-in-law wasted no time telling me as much.

When the doctor finally came out I had to tell them she was my wife in order to get information. She had a pretty good concussion, bruising, and cuts on her face. Her arm and leg were banged up too, but luckily no broken bones.

She's going to be really fucking sore for a while

but will make a full recovery. The plan is to keep her overnight just because of the concussion, and they want to have a handle on her pain.

I stand up and stretch my muscles, which are stiff from sleeping in the uncomfortable chair in the corner of Harley's hospital room. I walk over to the side of the bed and brush her hair out of her face. They said she'd have thin scars that would fade over time, but she's alive and that's all that matters.

I stare down at her when her eyes flutter open. "Hey," I whisper.

"Where am I?" She tries to sit up, but I grab her hand.

"No, baby, you need to lie down. Do you remember the accident?"

Harley closes her eyes. "A truck."

I nod. "The light was red, but you went right through it. I saw it happen."

She closes her eyes again. "The car?"

"What car, baby?"

Harley swallows. "The car following me. I-It hit me f-from behind. I was trying to get away."

My hackles rise. Then I remember the car that was right behind her—someone *intentionally* hit her? As soon as she's out, I need to make some calls.

"Am I okay?" Her question pulls me from my thoughts.

Do I tell her everything all at once? Yes; that's what I had wanted when I'd been shot and I woke up in the hospital in Germany. "You've got some cuts and bruises on your face. Your left side is banged up, and you've got a cracked rib and bruised sternum. You have a concussion, and due to how long it took you to wake up while they were examining you, they want to keep you overnight for observation."

I bring her hand up to my lips. "Are you in pain?" She nods, but then winces. "I'll go get the nurse."

***

I lift Harley out of my SUV and carry her toward my front door. Delilah opens it for me and smiles at Harley as I walk through the doorway with her.

Harley hadn't put up much of fight about coming back to my place to recuperate. I'm sure a lot of it is because she's scared—someone caused the accident, and she's super high on pain meds right now. Maybe it was a dick move to bring her to my home while she was under the influence, but she's got no one and I didn't want her to be alone—not until the police or my team find out who caused her accident.

I take her into my bedroom and lay her carefully on my bed. Delilah stacks some pillows at the end and carefully shoves them under Harley's sore leg. "Thanks, Del." Harley's words are slurred, but then her eyes close and she begins snoring softly.

"Can you sit with her while I go get her meds?" I ask. "I'm going to stop by her house, grab Fifty, her laptop, and some clothes."

Delilah climbs on my bed, sitting next to a sleeping Harley. "Go—we'll be fine. Don't forget some ice packs too."

I kiss my daughter on the head and leave to run all of my errands.

It takes me a few hours to get everything done, but by the time I'm finished I've got her pain meds, ice packs, clothes, and her damn bunny.

The moment I enter the house I hear voices. "I need to go home."

"Harley, you can't leave—you're hurt, and it's not safe. We just want to help you." There's silence for a moment. "I know my dad hurt you, but he can be kind of a dummy." I shake my head and smile. "Please let him do this and make things right. My mom did a number on him." I close my eyes because I hate that my daughter even knows that.

I move into the kitchen so I don't hear the rest of their conversation. My daughter is forever my cheerleader, but I can't let Becky's rotten behavior be a crutch or the reason I stay single. If I can get Harley to forgive me for being stupid, I can see us having a future together.

The night she helped me babysit, I watched from the door as she read to my granddaughter. The way she tenderly brushed Charlie's hair back before kissing her forehead showed me that she'd make a fantastic, loving mother.

While I get Fifty situated, I close my eyes and visualize her with a rounded belly, or cradling our child in her loving arms. Harley wouldn't use our child as a pawn...*Wait,* what am I thinking? It's way too soon to be thinking about kids. Hell, after the way I've treated her, I'm not sure she's going to take me back.

I make Harley and Del a sandwich and grab them

some chips and water. I head upstairs, and Delilah is still sitting next to Harley on the bed. "I made you guys some lunch."

"Thanks, Dad."

I hand them their food. "I got your pain pills." Harley looks up at me, and I hate seeing the swelling, bruises, and the cuts...but I hate seeing the blank look she's giving me even more. I shake two pain pills out of the bottle and place them on the nightstand next to her. "I want you to eat and then take these. At first you need to stay on top of the pain."

I walk to the door and turn. "I'll get you an ice pack for your face."

Harley says nothing but takes a bite of her sandwich...at least she's eating. I head downstairs and grab a beer out of the refrigerator. The hiss of the bottle as I twist the cap off is a comfort right now. It's going to take a *lot* to get her to trust me again. I'm going to have to earn my way back in.

***

It's been three days since I brought Harley back to my place to recover. She's been sleeping the majority of the time, but that's good because she's allowing herself time to heal. The swelling in her face is almost gone, and the bruises aren't as angry.

I'm still not making a lot of headway with her, but she at least has let me take care of her. I've kept her pretty much sequestered upstairs and in my bed. I've had to work some, though, so Delilah and Shayla have come over to help.

I think she's felt better having a woman help her shower. I've seen her naked, but I'm not surprised right now that she doesn't want me to see her that way.

Egan tried tracing the IP address of Martha's email, but they used a VPN to mask the real location. He's doing some more digging because Egan loves a challenge, but I was hoping that I'd have some good news for Harley by now.

Next week we've got a meeting with the manager for up-and-coming MMA star Becca McNeal. They want us to take care of her security detail while she trains in Chicago. Dalton is probably going to be my go-to guy for this. Normally we don't really do security for someone, but we make an exception in certain instances.

Her coach is an old friend of Marcus's. Apparently, this girl is so good that she's been attacked twice and has an obsessed fan. Her team wants round-the-clock coverage for her. Since Dalton is my martial arts expert, I figured he'd have the perfect cover—her sparring partner.

Today is my day at the office, and when I left home this morning, Shayla was sitting in bed with Harley and they were watching one of those vampire movies. I'm thankful for the women in my life. They're all so selfless and ready to help with anything.

That's what I wanted when I started Rogue—not only to build an amazing team, but a family.

After I pull into the parking garage, I take the elevator up to my floor. Carrie greets me from her post at the front desk. "Good morning, Jack. How's

Harley? Does she need anything?"

"I don't think she's going to need anything right now, and she's doing a little better today. The pain meds knock her out, but I want her to stay on top of the pain at least through the next couple of days."

"That must've been scary seeing the accident happen."

I've slept in my grandkids' bedroom since Harley's been at the house, which has been hard. Every bone in my body has screamed for me to sleep with her, but I don't want to until I can win her over again. My dreams have been more like nightmares the past three nights. I relive her accident over and over.

During each dream, when I reach her car I find her dead and then wake with a start. I end up rushing to check on her, and only once I see her safely sleeping in my bed am I able to relax enough to go back to sleep myself. "It was. Egan's going to check the cameras at that intersection. Harley said the car behind her bumped her a couple of times and she was trying to get rid of him."

"Oh wow, I can't believe it. Well, let me know if I can help with anything."

I nod and give a knock to her desk before I head back. I grab a cup of coffee in the break room and then head into my office.

It takes me most of the day to get caught up on phone calls and emails, and when I finish I call Shayla to check in on Harley.

"She's fine, Jack. We got her showered, and I changed the bedding. The sheets I stripped are in the dryer as we speak. I made Harley some lunch, gave her a pain pill, and now she's napping."

"Okay, thanks." I hang up and open the file on my desk.

On my way home from the office, I stop and get the stuff to make a homemade pizza. I pull into the garage and grab the bags, carrying them inside.

"Jack!" Erik and Shayla's son, Grant, comes racing toward me.

"What's up, little buddy?" Erik comes walking into the kitchen. "How's it going, Erik?"

He claps me on the shoulder. "Good, man—just came to look in on Harley and pick up my girl."

Shayla joins us with her and Erik's newborn, Chance, asleep in her arms. "Harley's asleep again. We got her follow-up with her family doctor scheduled for Friday."

I wrap my arm around her shoulders and give her a quick squeeze. "Great, thanks for sitting with her."

"Anytime, Jack. I can be here whenever you need now that I'm on maternity leave." I walk them to the door after Erik straps his tiny son into his little carrier. It's amazing that Erik went from ladykiller to father and a husband-to-be in such a short period of time. He's amazing with his kids—a natural.

Once they leave, I head upstairs and peek in on Harley. She's awake and staring at the TV. "Are you in any pain?"

She shakes her head but doesn't look at me.

With a sigh, I crawl on the bed and position myself right next to her. We're not touching, but we're close enough that I can feel the heat of her skin. "Listen, I know I fucked up. I told you I would, and I'm not making excuses, but I'm sorry. I'm *so* fucking sorry that I hurt you all because I was scared."

I scrub a hand over the top of my head. "My parents have been married for forty-five years. They love each other to this day just as fiercely as when they met. Mom almost died having me, so Dad put his foot down and said no to any more kids."

I glance at Harley and see she's finally looking at me. "In high school I dated…*a lot*. I was kind of a dog."

"I'm not surprised," Harley murmurs.

"I met Becky when I was eighteen, the summer after I graduated. She lived in the next city over. We were hot and heavy from the start, and I was playing baseball for the local community college. I was trying to get my GPA up so I could apply to the University of Iowa. Then she got pregnant with Del. Becky got pregnant on purpose, but then didn't want to have her. But I begged and begged her to have the baby."

I feel her put her hand on mine. "The best moment in my whole life was holding my newborn daughter in my arms. She was so tiny, but so heavy. I joined the Army when she was one. Needless to say, it was the hardest decision I ever made, but I wanted to make a difference. I wanted to provide for my daughter—to make her proud. During my time in the service, Becky and I divorced. When I decided to fight her for custody, she threatened to take my daughter and run if I tried to give Del to my parents.

"I will always hate that woman for the mental abuse she inflicted on our daughter, and then when she kidnapped her and tried to steal my granddaughter...that was the last straw."

Harley's quiet, but she hasn't let go of my hand. "I'm sorry that you and Delilah had to deal with that," she finally says. She rests her head on my shoulder. "But trusting you again is going to take time."

I nod, because there's nothing I can say. I'm just going to have to prove to her that I won't fuck up again, or at least not fuck up and break things off with her.

"Do you want to sit downstairs for a little bit? Maybe eat dinner outside, get some fresh air?" I climb off the bed, and at her nod, I scoop her up into my arms and carry her downstairs. In the kitchen, I set her down on her feet and hold her until she's steady.

Harley looks up at me. "You don't have to keep carrying me," she says softly.

"I know, but I want to." I watch her move through the kitchen and then into the living room. "Don't wear yourself out," I tell her as she keeps moving.

"Sorry, I'm just tired of sitting." Harley looks so cute when she pouts.

"Why don't you go sit outside? I'll be out in a minute." I open the door to the back deck and help her get settled in her chair.

"Thank you. Can you bring me my laptop? I need to check my emails and let my editor know what happened."

I kiss the top of her head and then head inside to get everything out for dinner. Then I bring her laptop to her.

While I make our pizza, I watch her through the kitchen window. I know I have a lot more to prove to her, but today I finally feel a little bit of hope.

Chapter Twelve

Harley

A week has gone by and things have slowly shifted with Jack and me. I don't know if I'm ready to trust him yet, but he's trying really hard. After the day when he laid it all out, I quit giving him the silent treatment. He's done so much for me—waiting on me hand and foot—even though I told him he didn't need to.

It's been so cute watching him as he takes care of Fifty. Jack acts like he doesn't like him, but he snuggles my bunny any chance he gets. We have switched venues though, and now we're staying at my place.

I was worried about his hip, with him constantly carrying me up and down the stairs. He relented when I told him he could stay with me if that made him feel better. The words were no sooner out of my mouth before he was heading upstairs to pack a bag.

Charlie's been over a lot because her papa is

here, and it's been nice—nice, but *loud*. The first day we came back, she came over with Del and they brought me flowers. Then Charlie had to kiss my owies because it would make them feel better.

The only bad thing is they weren't able to trace the email. Martha sent it from a dummy account, which Jack said they kind of expected, but he still seemed really pissed about it. Egan came over, and while he was installing my security system, he gave me his email to forward any more messages I get from her.

The car that was following me and bumping me was an older model Impala. From the video footage they couldn't tell if it was a man or a woman behind the wheel, and there were no plates visible so they were at loss. I, of course, never got a good look at the person, either.

I'll never tell anyone, but it's been so nice having Jack here, and not just because he makes breakfast and dinner for me every day or that he cleans up. I'm finding him very easy to talk to.

Now I'm in my office working on my story, trying to make up for last week. Luckily, I'm a plotter most of the time, so I know where my story is headed...it's just typing it all out and making sure it's not absolute garbage.

Today is my first day home alone, and so far, so good. I'm still sore and moving slowly, but definitely improving every day. I hear the front door open, then footsteps. Seconds later, Jack comes walking into my office. "What are you doing home already?" I ask.

Jack bends down and kisses me chastely on the

lips. "I had that meeting today."

"With the MMA fighter?"

"Yeah, Dalton's going to be her 'sparring partner.' She didn't seem thrilled about it, but it's the best way to get one of my guys close to her. Dalton was supposed to meet her today, but he was out with Marcus picking up a skip. Did you get some writing done?" He leans against my desk and looks down at me.

"I did. I don't know why, but it's kind of a blessing that I'm mostly immobile. I've gotten so much done."

"Any emails?" I shake my head. "That's good. Do you want to go out to dinner tonight? I figure you might want out of the house for a while."

"Yes—oh my God, a *hundred times yes*. I'm going stir crazy." He helps me stand, and I walk into my bedroom.

I change out of my sweat shorts and tank top and into some old, worn-out jeans that are threadbare in the knees but so comfortable. I pull on a red off-the-shoulder t-shirt and slip my feet into some flip-flops.

I took a shower this morning under Jack's watchful eye, and by the time I was done I was so turned on. I didn't miss the erection he had, but we both pretended that it wasn't there. I'm not ready to go back there, plus I'm still battling headaches. But luckily a half a pain pill at night and ibuprofen during the day is enough.

I walk out to the living room and find Jack sitting on the couch. He smiles when he sees me. "Are you feeling okay? Tired? Sore?"

I sit down next to him. "I'm good. I promise, Jack."

We decide to eat at Applebee's, which works for me. He talks to the hostess and gets us a table in the corner at the front of the restaurant so I won't have to weave my way through the crowded restaurant. I don't miss the way most of the women in this place are checking him out.

Jack's jeans mold to his thick thighs and perfect, David Beckham-worthy ass. The faded black Foo Fighters shirt molds to his lean but muscular chest. I really want to bite his bicep—wait...*what*? I shouldn't be thinking about that, at least not right now.

Once he gets me settled, he sits across from me. We order drinks and the waitress leaves us. "Thank you so much for this. I was starting to go a little cuckoo. I mean I know I'm at home a lot normally, but at least I had the choice if I wanted to leave or not."

He reaches across the table and grabs my hand. "You're welcome. I figured you could use a night out. Did you talk to the insurance company about your car?"

"Yeah, my car is totaled, obviously. They got the police report from the accident so I'm not at fault. Luckily there were enough witnesses to corroborate my story. They should be cutting me a check to replace it soon. Will you go with me?"

"Of course. Whatever you need from me."

I stare at him from across the table. I'm still in awe that this man wants me, and even though he hurt me I still want him and to give him another chance, but I'm scared. "Thank you...for everything." I shred my napkin, and then look up at him. "You hurt me before, but I get it. I'd like to give us another try."

The smile that graces his lips makes the already gorgeous man *stunning*. "That makes me so happy, baby. I promise I won't pull that shit I pulled before."

"I believe you, and I'm sorry I've given you the silent treatment."

He shakes his head. "You have no reason to apologize." Our waitress interrupts us when she comes to bring our drinks and takes our order.

When we finish dinner, we stop by the store and he runs inside to get stuff for ice cream sundaes. When we get home he pulls into the driveway and comes around to help me out. Inside I get situated on the couch while he tinkers around in the kitchen.

He comes in with a heaping bowl. "Oh my God, what's in the bowl?"

"It's a Mackenzie Deluxe: a scoop of vanilla with caramel sauce, a scoop of chocolate with chocolate sauce, and another scoop of vanilla with hot fudge, all topped with whipped cream." He hands me the bowl and I just want to shove my face in it.

"This looks amazing. I don't think I can eat all of this."

I look up as he sits down next to me. "That's because we're sharing."

That's exactly what we do—snuggle on the couch, eat our ice cream, and watch some college ballgame.

***

I lie on my side, and Jack is snuggled against my back with his arm around my waist. Since the night we went to dinner, things have *again* shifted between us. He kisses me a lot and snuggles me while we sleep.

Before he was sleeping on my couch, and at his place he slept in Charlie's bed. Now he's back in my bed, and I don't miss the hard dick that's poking my ass. I very slowly, very carefully, rub my butt against him. We haven't done anything more than kiss since I've decided to give him another chance, and I'm freaking horny.

His arm around my waist tightens, and a groan slips past his lips. My hair is in a ponytail, giving him unhindered access to my neck. Jack kisses me behind my ear and then nips my earlobe.

I reach behind me, gripping his hair in my fist as he kisses my neck and grinds against my ass. His hand around my waist slides down between my legs. I moan as he begins to strum my clit through my panties. "I've missed your pussy. It's so hot, wet, and so fucking sweet." I cry out as he pushes one finger inside me. "You're so responsive. Fuck, I wish I could strip you bare and fuck you."

My pussy clenches around his finger. "Please?" I'm begging and I don't care.

"Not yet, baby. You need to do some more healing, but let me make you come," he whispers against my neck.

"Okay," I moan.

He strums my clit, bites my neck, and grinds his

dick against me—that's all it takes to make me detonate. I cry out and pump my hips, riding the blissful wave. Jack brings me down slowly, I turn my head to kiss his lips, and then he moves us. I'm on my back and Jack's between my legs.

"You're so beautiful," Jack leans in and whispers against my lips. He reaches the nightstand and picks up his phone. "*Shit*, I've got to get up. I have a meeting today with a client and I can't be late." He carefully climbs off of me and then heads into the bathroom.

While he showers I make him a protein shake and start a pot of coffee. I head back into the bedroom and throw on a bra, t-shirt, and some cut-off sweats that I made. By the time I'm unlocking the door and Delilah and the kids are coming in, the cobwebs in my brain have cleared.

"Harley, go sit—I'll make you breakfast." I told Jack that I didn't need the girls to keep coming over and taking care of me, but he just pretended that he didn't hear me speak at all.

Charlie comes and sits next to me. "Hi sweetheart, should we watch cartoons?" The sweet little girl snuggles into me, and Jackson walks to us with his little arms held up. "You want to watch too?"

I pull him onto my lap, and we search through the menu until we hit the Disney Channel. I don't know what we're watching, but both kids are watching intently until Jack comes into the living room. "Papa!" Charlie slides off the couch and runs to him.

"Hi, my little nugget, are you here to help take

care of Harley?"

She nods, and her brown little pigtails bounce. "I am. I make her booboos not hurt."

He sets her down and comes over to me and Jackson. "Your shake is on the counter," I say. Jack bends down, kisses me, and picks Jackson up.

"Thanks, baby. How's my big boy?" Jackson babbles in his little baby talk, and it's the cutest thing ever.

They disappear into the kitchen, and I can hear Jack and Del talking. Before he leaves he kisses me one more time, and then he's gone.

When breakfast is ready, Delilah tries to bring my plate to me out in the living room, but I tell her I want to sit at the table. Once we sit down, we dig into our French toast. "How are you feeling?" I ask Del.

The petite blonde rubs a hand over her small swollen belly and smiles. "I feel great. I'm exhausted by the end of the day, but I feel great. This pregnancy has been the easiest one. Reece is such a big help, though—I'm so lucky." She takes a sip of her orange juice. "I know it's not my place, but I'm glad to see that things are better with you and my dad."

"Me too. We talked and he apologized, and I do want to try."

Del smiles and reaches out to grab my hand. "I think it's great. I know he can be a bootyhead, but he's the best dad a girl could ever ask for."

After breakfast she cleans up and refuses to let me help. The kids play with Fifty on the floor until Del gets the kitchen clean. "Okay, we're going to leave you to your writing. I'm off all day, so if you need anything just holler. Charlie, put Fifty back in his cage."

Once they're gone, I fill up my water bottle and grab my bag of snacks. In my office, I pull up my Word document and read through the last chapter to get myself back into the right headspace for my characters.

It isn't long until I'm immersed back into my characters' lives. By the time three o'clock rolls around, I can't sit any longer. I save my document and then get up, heading to the bedroom. I crawl onto the bed, and in no time, I fall asleep.

I bat whatever is tickling my face away, but it comes right back. I open my eyes and see Jack lying next to me. I smile up at him. "I fell asleep."

Jack smiles and leans into me, kissing my lips. "Did you get a lot done today?"

"I did. I'm ahead of schedule now. I wrote for five hours straight and was exhausted." He helps me sit up.

"Do you want to help me make dinner?" Jack asks. He wraps his arm around my shoulders as we head into the kitchen so I can help him cook. I pull up my Spotify app, and Heart starts playing through the speakers.

We work side by side in a companionable silence making baked ziti. While it's in the oven, we sit on the couch. "I hate that we didn't catch the fucker who was ramming your car. Any more emails from *Martha*?"

"No…do you think it was her that caused me to wreck?" I know Jack's pissed that they haven't caught her yet.

Jack shakes his head. "I want to say yes, but I just don't know."

The timer sounds, and we get up and head into the kitchen. I pull the salad out of the refrigerator and pop the garlic bread under the broiler.

When the sides are done, I carry them to the table and Jack fills our plates, sitting mine in front of me. He takes his place across from me. "Egan thinks he may have found where the emails originated from."

"That's great. What will you do if you find it? Find her?" I take a bite of the pasta.

Jack sets his fork down. "I'll follow her around, see what her story is. Make sure it's her."

"Okay. I never asked how much I owe you for tracking her down."

He shakes his head. "I don't want your money. This is something I wanted to do for you. Don't try to sneak money to any of my team, either. I've given them explicit instructions to ignore you."

"But I have the money."

Jack gets up and comes around to my side, squatting down in front of me. "I know you have the money, but as your man this is something I need to do. I protect what's mine."

Why does that turn me on? I bite my lip and nod. "Okay, I won't try to pay anyone…promise."

He leans into me, kissing me quickly before sitting across from me again. When we finish eating, he doesn't let me clean up, either. Instead I sit in the living room holding Fifty, whose lazy ass is fast asleep on my lap.

Once Jack is done, he joins me on the couch. He situates us where my head is resting on his lap, and my legs are propped up on the arm. While Jack watches some documentary about sharks, I zone out and just chill.

I can't remember the last time I vegged out with someone else, especially like this, and I really, really like it. I like it so much it scares me, but just like Jack is, I'm trying to power through my fear.

When Jack's show is over, he oversees my shower…he's afraid I'm going to pass out or something. There's never been anything I've done more intimate than when he helps me shower. We've got our routine down, that's for sure. I strip out of my clothes and throw my robe on.

He lifts me into the bathtub—see? He babies me—then I shrug off my robe. "Are you washing your hair?" I shake my head. Jack soaps up a washcloth and begins scrubbing my body.

This is a completely nonsexual thing, but I'm completely turned on right now. In slow circular motions, he rubs the soap onto my body. He even tries to shave my armpits and my legs, but I swat at him. When I'm done he shuts off the water and lets me dry myself off…surprisingly.

Back in my bedroom, I sit on the end of my bed and rub my lavender and chamomile lotion into my skin. I throw my nightgown on sans panties and climb back on the bed, settling with my back against the stack of pillows leaned against my headboard.

I hear the shower kick on and in my mind's eye I can picture the water sluicing down Jack's body. I lean back against the pillows and close my eyes as I imagine licking the water off of his muscled chest.

I listen closely and hear the water still running. Reaching between my legs, I moan softly as my fingers brush over my clit. While I rub it in tiny circles, I imagine running my hands all over Jack's wet body. I bite my lip as I slip my fingers through my wetness, and then rub it over my clit.

It doesn't take long before I'm on the verge of coming. I imagine getting down on my knees, wrapping my hand around his big, beautiful cock. In my mind I imagine the way his dick stretches my mouth as he grips my hair, fucking my mouth.

I pump my hips as my orgasm begins to build. I jump when I feel a hand wrap around my wrist. Opening my eyes, I find Jack staring down at me. "You don't come without me."

He moves between my legs, kissing the insides of both of my thighs. I moan as he begins to lick me. Jack sucks my clit into his mouth, pushes one finger inside, and I come embarrassingly fast.

I sigh. "Oh, *wow*."

Jack moves up the bed and lies next to me. The towel wrapped around his waist leaves nothing to the imagination, and he's rock hard. I hold his eyes as I reach over, undoing his towel and wrapping my hand around his dick.

He grunts from deep in his throat, and that spurs me on. I increase my speed and grip, and Jack doesn't look away. This is the most erotic thing I've ever done. When he begins to come he moans, his eyes rolling back.

Jack leans into me. "That was amazing." He

kisses me. "You're a naughty girl." His words are whispered against my lips. He cleans himself off with his towel and tosses it on the floor.

"Well, quit being so hot," I whisper back.

His chuckle vibrates against my chest, and he wraps his arm around my shoulders. We settle in, and it isn't long before I feel myself start to fall asleep.

Chapter Thirteen

Jack

I follow closely behind the man that looks like an older, male version of Harley. She didn't ask me to find him, but I wanted to do this for her. To be honest he was easy to find, and if Harley really wanted to find him, she could've.

He lives in a high-rise downtown, he's married, and Harley's got a younger sister that looks just like her. From what I found out she's eight years younger than Harley. My stomach turned the moment I found that out.

The asshole dumped his kids with their grandma and split, yet he created himself a whole new family while Harley lost everyone and is now all alone. Well, she's not alone any longer—she's got me.

Her dad walks into Shaw & Smith Realty and I just keep walking by—the man none the wiser that I'd been following him for the past five blocks. A big part of me wants to confront the deadbeat who walked out on Harley, but then I'd have to tell her what I did and I don't want to hurt her like that.

I head to the office, and when I reach our floor Carrie smiles at me from the front desk where she sits and talks on the phone. Every time I step into the back I'm always hit with a sense of pride. We worked hard to get to where we are.

In the break room I grab a bottle of water and run into Reece on my way back to my office. "What's up, Jack?"

"Not much. Do you have a second?" He follows me into my office, shutting the door behind him. "I found Harley's dad."

Reece doesn't say anything at first. "You're not smiling...am I to assume that it's not good?"

"Her dad remarried about a year after he dumped her and her brother. He started a new fucking family. Harley's got a younger half-sister."

"Wow...*shit*. Do you want Del there when you tell her?"

I shake my head. "She doesn't know I looked for him. I wanted to do something for her, but now I don't want to tell her."

"I don't know what to tell you. She might not be happy that you were poking around in her business. The information you have could hurt her. Is that what you want?"

I shake my head. "So what you're saying is I fucked up?"

"Yep. Sorry, man."

I knew it before I did it, but I looked anyway. "Okay, I won't tell her anything unless she asks me to find him."

Reece leaves and I call the head of security at

Litchfield Financial Group. They think their COO is stealing money from the company, and he's been skimming small amounts, but recently started getting more and more greedy.

I hold the phone to my ear while it rings. "Jack Mackenzie, how the fuck are you?"

"I'm good, Tom. I just wanted to update you on what we've found. First, I just want to say that this guy is a dipshit. He's been taking more and more this past month. My courier is bringing over all the information you need to fire and press charges against him."

Before we hang up, I send the invoice and ask him to follow up with me once they make their move.

The rest of the day is spent calling clients and checking in to make sure they're happy with our services. Delilah volunteered to make those calls, but I think it's a little more personal if I do it.

There's a knock on my office door, and Egan sticks his head in. "You got a second?"

I signal to him to come in while I finish my call. As soon as I hang up, I turn to Egan. "Do you have some news?"

"Yep, I finally got a lock on the email: It was sent using an IP address owned by a Sara and Justin Nelson in Indianapolis, but I don't think either of them sent it. Their IP address could've easily been stolen. Someone would just need to be near their home." He hands me a file. "They're newlyweds, and from the digging I've done, they seem to be a social couple who have lots of friends and are close with their families."

I flip through the folder and see screenshots from their social media profiles. They're a good-looking couple. He's a teacher and she's a nurse—I'm thinking that Egan's right about this one. It's not them, but fuck, it'd be nice if it was—then we could close this case.

"I'm not going to give up, and next time she gets an email, I want her forwarding it to us ASAP," Egan says. "I also think the next time she gets one she should respond."

I lean back in my chair. "Are you fucking kidding me?" Egan shakes his head. "It could've been Martha that caused Harley to get into her accident. Couldn't that enrage this person? Maybe cause them to react more violently?"

"Yes, but...if they make a move, we'd have a better chance at catching them. Harley would be completely safe—you're basically living together, and Reece is right next door. She's safe."

"I'll talk to her—see where her head's at. What's she supposed to say?"

"Nothing negative, just maybe an, 'I'm sorry you feel that way.' If Harley sympathizes with *Martha*, then maybe she'll stop sending her the emails and won't destroy any more of Harley's books."

I nod. "I'll talk to her."

At three o'clock, I stop by Del's office before leaving for the day. "Hey, honey. How's it going?"

She smiles up at me. "Hey Dad, it's going good. Just sending out invoices and paying some bills."

"Great, I'm heading home."

I turn to walk out, but Del stops me. "Dad?" I turn to look back at her. "I'm really happy that

Harley forgave you for being a dope." I bark out a laugh. "What? You *were* a big old dope, but I love you. I love her for you."

Delilah comes around her desk and wraps her arms around me. "Thank you, baby girl." I kiss her forehead and rub a hand over her swollen belly.

I pull into the driveway, hop out of my SUV, and make my way to the front door. I pull out the set of keys that Harley gave me and unlock the door, stepping inside. It's quiet—almost too quiet. "Harley?" I call, but she doesn't answer.

First, I look outside and don't see her. Next, I head through the house and look in her office—it's empty. Last, I head into her bedroom and find her asleep again. I move around to the side of the bed and sit down.

I reach out, brushing her hair out of her face. Her eyes flutter open and she gives me that sleepy grin that I'm growing to love. "Hi," she says, her voice thick with sleep.

"Hey, baby. How was your day?"

She covers her mouth as she yawns. "It was good. I fell asleep again. I swear I don't nap this much."

"You're healing from the accident. Of course you're going to be tired. Do you want to go see a movie?" She nods. "How about we go to the multiplex? They serve food."

While she gets ready, I look up movie times and decide to take her to see the new disaster flick. She said that they're a guilty pleasure of hers. It doesn't start for another hour, so we have plenty of time. Ten minutes later, she comes out in a pair of cut-off jean shorts, a black t-shirt, and a baggy red cardigan.

Her hair is in one of those knots on top of her head, and her face is free of makeup. She's so beautiful she takes my breath away. I don't deserve her, but I don't care anymore.

After the movie, I shake my head as Harley wipes the tears from her eyes. "Are you going to be okay?" I try to keep the humor out of my voice, but I can't help it.

Harley looks at me all disgruntled. "He loved her, and sacrificed himself to save her and their baby." The tears spill over again, and I pull her into a hug.

"It's just a movie."

I know it's the wrong thing to say when she pushes back. "*Just* a movie? *Seriously*?" The couple behind us chuckle as they walk by.

"You're right, I'm sorry."

With a huff, she stands up. We head out to my SUV and I help her get loaded into it. I grab her hand and hold it while we make our way back home.

After getting her settled on the couch, I make us a couple of sundaes. The doorbell rings, and I tell her I've got it. I smile when I open the door. My granddaughter stands on the other side, waving wildly. "Papa, I come see you."

I push open the screen door and she comes running in, followed by Reece. "Hey guys, she saw you pull into the driveway and wanted to come say goodnight."

Charlie is curled up on the couch next to Harley

in her little *Peppa Pig* nightgown. Her brown hair hangs down her back in two braids. I smile at her and then turn to Reece. "Is Jackson in bed already?"

"Yeah, he is. Del fell asleep too. Charlie and I were watching *Sportscenter* snuggled up on the couch when we saw you pull in."

They stay long enough for me to get some snuggles from my little nugget. Harley invites her to spend the night during the upcoming weekend, and she's super excited about it. While Harley disappears down the hall to use the bathroom, I walk Charlie and Reece out.

"I'm happy for you, Jack. Harley's really great." He claps me on the shoulder before he scoops up his daughter and carries her home.

I step back inside and sit down on the couch next to Harley. "Charlie can always stay with me at my place if you think it'll be too much having a three-year-old here."

"I wouldn't have offered if I didn't want her to stay. Maybe we can make those homemade pizzas?"

I kiss her forehead. "Thanks, baby. That's a great idea."

***

I flip through the magazine in the waiting room while Harley is in the back for her last post-accident checkup. I had to take a call when we got here, so I let her go back without me.

Things have been going great with Harley and me. Since she's doing much better she doesn't really need me, but I need to ensure she's safe so

I've still been staying with her. It's just this unspoken thing between us, but every night I sleep with her snuggled against my chest, and I know I don't want to leave.

Harley hasn't gotten any emails lately, but she told me that sometimes there would be huge gaps when she wouldn't get any. There have been no mysterious deliveries either. It makes me a little nervous and keeps me on edge, but I try to play it cool. There's no need to freak her out.

We found out that Delilah's having another boy, and I'm fucking thrilled that Charlie's getting another brother to watch over her and protect her. My daughter is sublimely happy right now, and I'm happy for her. She deserves to live in her happy little bubble.

Business has been great. We haven't seen much of Dalton at the office since he's doing that security detail. I know he's been butting heads with Ms. McNeal, but he's at least doing his job. I know I'll owe him big when this job is over.

The door opens and my attention goes to my girl, who comes walking through it. She stops at the desk and talks to the receptionist.

I stand up and meet her up at the desk. "The payment plan will start today and then we'll bill you monthly," the receptionist tells Harley.

"Okay, thank you," she says and then smiles up at me.

I wrap my arm around her shoulders and lead her outside to my SUV.

Harley's been afraid to drive since the accident, and I understand that, but I know she'll feel better when she can come and go as she pleases. She's at least picked up her new ride, a brand-new blue Camry with all the bells and whistles. I will admit it's a sweet ride and handles like a dream.

"How was your appointment?" I pull into this little hole-in-the-wall Mexican restaurant for lunch before I'll take her home and head back to the office.

"It was good. I'm just glad my ribs and my head no longer hurt."

Inside the restaurant, we seat ourselves in a little booth by the door. The waiter drops off chips and salsa and takes our drink order. I watch Harley attack them with gusto. My girl loves her food. "Do you have anything you want to do tonight?" I ask her before grabbing a chip of my own.

"I wish it wasn't getting chilly because I want to go swimming."

"I keep it warm enough that we'll be fine, so we'll swim tonight. In another couple of weeks, I'll close it down until next spring."

"Really?" She claps and bounces up and down in her seat. "That's great! I can't wait to get into the water."

"Okay, tonight we'll stay at my house and after dinner we can go for a swim. That'll be good." I can't wait to get her in her little bikini again.

Chapter Fourteen

Harley

My legs are wrapped around Jack's hips as he thrusts into me over and over. I know I've got to be hurting him the way I'm gripping his hair, but I don't think he cares. Jack reaches between us, strumming my clit until I'm close to detonating.

"Fuck me, but you feel amazing," he whispers against my neck. "Are you going to come for me?"

"Yes…now…" I come long and hard, and I know I'm a wet mess, but I feel too good to care. Jack pumps once, twice, and then buries himself to the hilt as he begins to come. I wrap my arms around him, hugging Jack to my chest. He pulls out as his dick starts softening.

He kisses me once before climbing out of the bed and disappearing into his bathroom. I grab his pillow and hug it to my chest, smiling.

Earlier today I worked a little on my book while Jack hung out with his daughter and the kids. I got excited because a signing downtown had a spot open up, so I'm getting to attend now. I paid my fees and when they announced me, I was excited to see people were actually excited that I was going to be there.

Maybe Jack and I could get a hotel room and make it a romantic weekend away. My happy bubble was burst, though, when I went through the rest of my emails and found one from Martha.

> Eva,
> I was hoping after your little "accident" that you'd stop that vulgar writing, but I've seen your posts on social media, bragging about your new book. You're turning women into whores with your pornography.
> 1 John 1:9
> If we confess our sins, he is faithful and just to forgive us our sins and to cleanse us from all unrighteousness.
> Confess before it's too late. God will forgive you like he's forgiven me.
> Martha

I was surprised when Jack said they wanted me to placate her and apologize, but that's just because they want her to make a move, and that makes me nervous. They're the experts, though, so I should trust their judgment.

I forward the email to Egan with the question, "What do I say to her?" When I finish with the other emails, I check the ads I have running constantly on Facebook. I've spent a fortune on marketing classes, but it was worth it.

I email my editor letting her know that I'll be sending my manuscript at the end of next week. It'll go through one more round of edits and a proofreader before it's ready to get formatted, and still there are sometimes tweaks that need to be made.

My release is set for seven weeks from now. Things will get crazy while I prepare for release day, but I'm used to it. Of course I still get release day jitters, and I'm sure I always will. Most authors I talk to say they still get them too.

For dinner tonight we ate with Del, Reece, and the kids. Charlie is obsessed with looking me over for more owies—I think she's going to be a doctor or a nurse. The kids were in rare form and made me smile constantly. Delilah had music playing, and both kids were dancing for us. It was adorable and made me long for children of my own.

Jack and I haven't had *the us* talk yet, but I hope we're on the same page because I'm falling in love with the man. I can see a future with us, but I'm scared because for so long everyone I've ever loved has always left me.

We stayed at their house until the kids went to sleep, and that brings us back to now. It had been since before my accident that we'd last had sex, and when we became us again we've only done oral or hand jobs.

I wasn't sure if I should make the move or see if he was going to make it. In the end I threw caution to the wind and stripped out of all of my clothes, lying there waiting for him. When he came into the room, he froze. In seconds he came unstuck and was shucking off his t-shirt and then his jeans.

He'd basically tackled me in bed.

Now he's situating us so I'm lying half on and half off him. My fingers draw imaginary circles on his chest. "I forgot to tell you that I'm doing a signing next month downtown. They had an author cancel and I was the next in line."

"That's great, baby."

"Will you come with me? I thought maybe we could get a room downtown and have a romantic weekend." I rest my chin on top of my folded hands and look at him in the dark.

"Just admit it—you want me to come be one of those cover models. You know, stand behind you and flex," he says, making me laugh.

"Har, har…that's not even how it is, but yeah, you can just sit there and look pretty." Jack tickles my sides until I'm squealing. "Okay, s-stop!"

"Egan showed me the email," Jack says quietly. I was expecting him to ask me about it earlier tonight. "I don't think I'm ready for you to reply yet. Things could escalate rapidly, and I need to get a lot more things in place before you do that."

"I wasn't thrilled about responding anyway. I won't until you tell me to."

He hugs me tightly, and it isn't long before he's asleep, and I follow after him.

***

I take a drink of my coffee as I stare at the email on my laptop. How am I supposed to respond to this? She hasn't emailed this close together before, either.

> Dearest Eva,
> 1 Corinthians 6:18-20: Flee from sexual immorality. All other sins a person commits are outside the body, but whoever sins sexually, sins against their own body. Do you not know that your bodies are temples of the Holy Spirit, who is in you, whom you have received from God? You are not your own; you were bought at a price. Therefore honor God with your bodies.
> I know you're taking up with that man I've seen you with. Sex before marriage is a sin. Not only do you write that filth, but now you're being intimate with a man you're not married to.
> Your punishment is coming, mark my words.
> Yours in Jesus,
> Martha

I grab my phone and call Jack. He answers on the second ring. "Hey baby, what's up?"

"Um...Martha emailed again. I know you guys want me to email her, but I don't think I want to email her back." I take a deep breath. "She knows about you."

I may not be in the same room as Jack, but the silence is very telling—he's pissed. "What do you mean she knows about me?" I read him the entire email and he cusses quite a bit. "Are the doors locked?"

"I think so." I bite at my thumbnail and stare out the window.

"Go check them while we're on the phone." My heart starts to beat faster as I rush through the house to the front door and flip the deadbolt. At the backdoor, I flip that lock too. "Are they locked?"

"Yes, I'm really freaked out right now. Is she watching me? Is she watching us?"

"Pack your bags, get Fifty ready, and when I'm done here I'll come get you. We'll stay at my place. I have a state-of-the-art security system."

"Okay. I'll be ready when you get home."

He's quiet for a moment. "Baby, listen to me. You're safe, okay?"

I *do* believe him…or at least I want to. "She knows who I really am, she knows about you…*how*?"

"Forward me the email so I can get it to Egan. Cobi has already said he'd watch that couple if I changed my mind. I know we ruled them out, but I just need to be sure."

After we hang up I can't focus on anything else, and I can't just sit and watch TV or read, so I clean my place from top to bottom. When Jack gets home, I'm knee deep in reorganizing my closet.

"What are you doing? You probably shouldn't be on the floor, baby." He helps me stand up. "Did you pack?" *God,* he's overprotective.

I shake my head. "Earlier I couldn't sit still, and I couldn't focus on anything. I decided to start cleaning and I went a little crazy, I'll admit. Can you get Fifty's stuff together while I pack?"

I watch him disappear out the door.

It takes me about a half hour to get clothes, toiletries, and my writing stuff all together. I wheel my suitcase out into the living room and find Jack in the kitchen with his phone to his ear. "I'm bringing her to my place." He pauses. "Yes, come. We'll throw a shower for Delilah and you can meet Harley. Mom, I'm forty-three years old—I think I can handle putting a party together for my daughter." Jack turns and holds out his hand to me. "Fine, you plan her party, but I'm paying." He smiles. "Okay, we'll see you in a couple of weeks." Jack kisses the top of my head. "I love you too."

He disconnects the call. "My daughter spilled the beans about us, so my mom was pumping me for information. Don't worry: If you don't want to meet them, you don't have to. My mom's just a little protective."

"Umm…sure, I'd love to meet them…unless *you* don't want me to." I pull back and look up at him.

"Of course I do. Do you have all your stuff together?" I nod, and he takes my suitcase out to his SUV before returning for Fifty. I make sure everything is locked up and follow Jack. Once we're both inside, we head to his place.

After getting Fifty situated, I head upstairs to put my clothes away, and then Jack takes me into his office. He rearranges his desk so I have room to work. "You didn't have to do this. I feel bad enough that you have to babysit me."

Jack moves around the desk until he's standing right in front of me. "You haven't made me do anything. I don't call it babysitting—I call it taking care of someone that I care a lot about." I know it's not a declaration of love, but it still feels really good.

I wrap my arms around his waist. "Thank you so much." I let go of Jack's waist and grab his face, pulling him down to me for a fierce kiss. "You're an amazing man, Jack Mackenzie."

He lifts me up and sets me on the desktop. Jack spreads my legs and fits himself between them. He brushes my hair out of my face. "You are so, so pretty."

I feel my face heat up. "Thank you. What should we have for dinner?" I grab onto his shoulders.

"Do you want to order out, or go somewhere?"

"I'd rather stay in, if you don't mind?"

We order Chinese and while we wait for it to come, Jack teaches me to play chess. I'm actually surprised that he plays. His dad taught him when he was a kid, and he started playing again when he was in the hospital after he got shot.

I listen as he tells me about the pawns, rooks, knights, bishops, queens, and kings. I'll admit I don't understand half of what he's saying, but the first game we play he helps me. It's actually a lot more fun than I thought it would be.

When our food comes we continue playing while we eat. It's safe to say I'm terrible at chess because I'm losing pieces faster than I know what to do with. Jack gets up to get a beer and me a glass of wine. "When did your parents move to Florida?"

"The minute my dad retired from John Deere, they were gone. My mom runs a bookstore in Panama City Beach. If my daughter would stop popping out babies, I want to take them down there for a vacation."

I smack his arm. "*Stop*...you know you love those babies."

"I do. I remember when she told me she was pregnant with Charlie. I was so pissed and didn't react well, but I went to that first appointment and heard the heartbeat and I was over the moon. I wasn't happy at first when I found out Reece was the dad. It wasn't that he wasn't a good guy—we served together, and he was always a good friend, but she was too young for him."

He takes a drink of his beer. "Luckily it all worked out. He'd die for her and those kids." Jack clears his throat. "Do you want kids?"

How do I answer that? How do I tell him I've always wanted a house full of babies, but that my fears keep me from thinking that'll ever be a possibility? Everyone I love leaves me, and I know I need to stop thinking that way, but I can't help it. I don't say anything, though—I just shake my head.

"Why?"

I don't want to talk about this, and I don't want to admit to him that I'm afraid. He'll think I'm pathetic like John, my last boyfriend, did. All I can think is *lie, lie, lie*. "I don't know...I just haven't been with someone I'd want to have babies with. I figure I've missed my shot." I stand up. "I'm going to get more wine. Do you want another beer?"

In the kitchen I grab our drinks and bring them back into the living room, sitting back down in front of the chessboard. Jack grabs my arm. "I only asked because I don't want more kids."

Why does that hurt? Instead, I push it away and smile. "Okay then, we're on the same page. Let's finish this game." He looks at me closely. Can he tell it's all lies?

Jack takes a drink of his beer. "Yeah baby, let's finish it."

Chapter Fifteen

Jack

"I wanted to bring something to the table that's been on my mind a lot lately." I look around the table at each member of my team—each one hand-selected by me. "I've been thinking about expanding. The space next door is available, and I've spoken to the contractor who did this space. He said we'd be able to do it."

I take a sip of my water. "We'd start hiring just a couple of guys first. Marcus, my hope is to get you a couple more bounty hunters. Shayla works with you a lot more, so she'd be in charge of keeping track of all your cases."

Marcus glances at Erik with a mischievous grin. "Your wife's going to be *all* mine."

"You couldn't handle my girl, pussy." Erik was the cocky dog until Shayla and Grant came into his life. Now he's a devoted husband—*finally*—and father.

I end the meeting and the guys all get up except

for Reece. "What's up?"

"Not much. Del's excited for Jerry and Kim to get here."

"They're excited too. My mom's been talking to yours about the baby shower for baby boy." Reece's chest always puffs out when his upcoming son is brought up. Then he rolls his eyes. "I can only imagine the spectacle they're going to turn it into, but Del deserves it. This pregnancy is wearing her out already, but she keeps smiling. Your daughter's a robot," he says with a laugh.

"Nah…she just loves being a mom," I tell him.

We head out of the conference room and I grab a bottle of water before heading back to my office. Earlier today Cobi emailed me some of his surveillance photos of the couple that owns the IP address where Harley's emails have been coming from. They're your basic couple: They go to work, sometimes out to dinner, she grocery shops, they hang with friends, and on Sundays they go to church.

Now that would raise red flags all over the place, but Cobi said it's one of those super-relaxed churches. He even said that there appears to be no abuse going on, but he said he'd do more digging.

Harley's been a little quiet since I moved her in with me. A part of me thinks she's just worried about Martha, but then again, the way she shut down after our brief discussion about kids has me thinking that's it.

She's still been affectionate with me and the sex has been phenomenal, but it's like she's keeping me at arm's length. Yesterday she finally took her new car out for a drive. I'd gone with her, and Harley got really nervous going through intersections or if someone was following us too closely, but I was so proud of her because she did it anyway.

I shut down my computer and decide to stop by to say hi to the kids. As soon as I pull into Del's driveway, I look over at Harley's house and the hairs on the back of my neck stand up. I climb out of my SUV.

"Hey, Dad." Del waves from the front steps.

I move toward her. "I'll be right back—I need to check Harley's house really quick."

Across the yard, I head toward the back of Harley's house. I look around and don't see anything unusual in the yard. The windows at the back of the house are still locked. I check the sliding door, and that's still locked too.

Once I move around the other side of the house, I examine the ground. Right in front of her bedroom window, the grass is depressed. I pull my phone out of my pocket and snap a few pictures.

I send a quick text to Del and ask her to bring me a bottle of baby powder. She meets me at the fence. "What's this for?"

"Nothing you need to worry about, honey. I'll be over to see you guys in a few minutes." I head back to the other side of the house. At the window, I grab my little kit out of my back pocket. I sprinkle some baby powder in my hand and use my little brush.

I find nothing, but I still don't feel right. Someone was here snooping around. I was hoping to find a fingerprint or at least a partial, but I couldn't get that lucky. I use the keys that she gave me when I was staying here with her and step inside.

I turn off the alarm system and do a quick walk-through, but I don't see anything out of order. In her bedroom I look around, and everything is how she left it. I arm the system and lock up.

"Papa!" Charlie calls from her timeout chair as I step into their house. "I was bad."

Jinx greets me with a bark, and I bend down to pet him and notice his hair is sticky. "Your granddaughter thought the dog needed a bath, and instead of shampoo, she used a gallon of milk," Delilah says as she blows a stray strand of hair out of her face. "I can't lift him enough to get him in the tub to wash it off, so we're waiting for Daddy to get home."

"I'll take care of the dog. Where's Jackson?"

"He's in his crib while I cleaned up the mess." She holds up the baby monitor in her hand.

I pick up Jinx, carry him upstairs to the bathroom, and stick the dog in the bath. In no time, the milk is rinsed off and he's all clean.

When I head back downstairs, Reece is home and Charlie is pouting on the couch. My grandson runs to me and I scoop him up in my arms. "How's my boy?" Jackson babbles his baby talk.

"Papa, I your nugget." Charlie's got her little arms crossed and a scowl on her face.

"Yes, you're my nugget, and you need to be a good girl for your mommy and daddy. That would make your papa very happy." Her little chin wobbles, but Reece scoops her up and throws her over his shoulder and then she's squealing.

LEAD SECURITY

I kiss the grandbabies and my daughter goodbye, then head back to my place.

When I step inside, I'm hit with the most amazing smell. In the kitchen, I find Harley stirring something in a pan. "Hey, honey." She greets me with a bright smile on her face.

I come up behind her, resting my hands on her shoulders. I bend down and kiss her when she tips her head back. "What's cooking? It smells amazing."

"It's just spaghetti, but I made the sauce from scratch. Garlic bread is in the oven, and the salad is in the refrigerator."

I squeeze Harley's shoulders and then kiss the top of her head. "That sounds great. I'm going to get washed up, and then I'll set the table."

Now Harley is acting like her normal self. Before, it must've been from being nervous about Martha. Now she's telling me all about her latest story and that she's got an idea for a military romance. "Would you answer questions for me? I want it to be authentic."

"Of course."

"Thank you, and I know there's stuff you can't tell me and maybe even stuff you don't want to talk about, so I'll take whatever information you give."

After we finish eating, we work side by side cleaning up the kitchen and spend the rest of the evening snuggled up on the sectional watching TV. In no time, Harley is asleep with her head on my shoulder.

***

I wake Harley when I'm done watching the news and she sleepily walks up the stairs. After shutting everything down and locking up, I head upstairs as Harley comes out of the bathroom and kiss her before she disappears into my bedroom.

After I take care of business I head into the bedroom. I smile as I watch Harley slip on one of my t-shirts, skimming over her curves. She's not wearing any panties, and I just want to bite her cheeks.

I come up behind her, wrapping my arms around her waist. "You look so fucking sexy in my t-shirt and no panties, but it was kind of a waste because I want you naked." I slide my hands up under her t-shirt, lifting it until it's on the floor next to the bed.

I grab her hair in my fist, moving it to the side. I lean down, kissing her neck slowly, just the way she likes it. Her skin is so warm and soft. I continue kissing and nipping at her neck—her nipples harden and I watch her chest rise and fall.

I yank her head back, attacking her lips more roughly than I intended, but she brings out the animal inside of me. She moans into my mouth as she tries to turn in my arms, but I don't let her. With my free hand I palm her breast, squeezing it before tweaking her nipple.

I give her other breast the same treatment before my hand slides down her stomach until I reach her wet cunt. I rub her clit, and she starts whimpering and writhing against me. I pull my mouth away from hers. "Are you going to come for me like a good girl?"

"Yessss…" she moans. I push one finger, then

two inside of her, biting her earlobe when she squeezes my fingers.

I work her over until she's drenching my hand. I pull my fingers from her, rubbing her swollen clit until she begins to cry out. I push my fingers back inside her as she explodes. Hearing Harley moan my name makes me hard as a rock, and my cock aches to be inside her.

With quick movements I toss Harley on the bed, strip out of my clothes, and then I'm over her. I grab my dick, rub it through her wet folds, and thrust inside her. Every time it's just like sinking into heaven.

I grab the underside of each of her thighs, pushing her legs wide—allowing me to sink further inside of her. "Fuck baby, you're like a fucking dream."

I pull almost all the way out before slamming back into her to the hilt, again, and again. Harley cries out over and over. I let go of one of her thighs and grab onto the headboard as I feel her pussy start to contract around me.

As she begins to come, I pick up the pace to almost brutal thrusts—I plant myself deep inside her as I begin to come hard, and that's when I realize I don't have a condom on, but it's too late now. I rest my head on Harley's chest and she wraps her arms around me.

"Baby?" I pull my softening dick out of her.

"Hmm..." she answers.

I take a deep breath. "I forgot a condom. I promise I'm negative for everything—it's been a couple of years for me, and I was tested a while ago. Are you on birth control?"

Harley shakes her head, and my stomach sinks. "I haven't really had a need for it, but my period's due next week so we'll be fine. Maybe I should go on the pill? Maybe I should get Plan B?"

"That's up to you, baby. I'll buy it since it was my fault. I *do* love the idea of being bare inside you."

She runs her fingers through my hair. "I'll make an appointment to get on the pill."

I smile down at her. "Let me get you cleaned up." In the bathroom I grab a wet washcloth to wipe myself off and grab another one that I take into the bedroom to wipe Harley off with—even though she tries to smack my hands away from her.

I toss it into the laundry basket and get us situated in bed so her back is snug against my front, and almost immediately she does that little hitch in her breath right before she softly snores.

As I hold her, all I can think about is I'm falling in love with her, and it scares the shit out of me, but I won't run from her ever again. I'm afraid if I do, she'd never give me another chance.

Chapter Sixteen

Harley

My palms sweat as I stand next to Jack by luggage claim waiting for his parents, whose flight just landed. I've been a nervous wreck, but thankfully I finished my book so that's one thing I'm no longer thinking about.

Charlie came with us and she holds my hand while twirling around. She's wearing adorable leggings with unicorns on them, a rainbow tutu, a light purple t-shirt, and hot pink Converse. Delilah warned us that Charlie dressed herself because she wanted to look "*bootiful.*"

"Relax, baby. They're going to love you," Jack whispers in my ear.

"Ummm…who is the last woman your parents met?" I know after Becky he hasn't had any serious relationships.

"Okay, touché, but you have the glowing approval of their only grandchild. They're going to love you." He kisses the top of my head. "Oh, here they come."

I see a couple walking toward us with huge smiles on their faces. Charlie squeals, "Nana and Pop Pop!" She lets go of my hand and runs right toward them.

Jack's dad is exactly what I expect Jack to look like in about twenty years. His mom is gorgeous: she's petite with brown hair that hangs down to her shoulders. She definitely doesn't look old enough to have a son in his early forties.

They come toward us smiling, his dad with Charlie on his hip. Jack lets go of me and goes to his mom, wrapping her in a bear hug and lifting her off the ground. "Put me down before you hurt yourself." Jack listens to his mother and sets her down. She pulls his face down, kissing both cheeks. "My boy is so handsome."

I smile because Jack—Mr. "Boss Man, ex-Special Forces"—is totally blushing. "Mom, seriously, I'm forty-three. I'm not a boy.

"You'll always be *my* boy." She kisses his cheek again and lets him go so she can take Charlie from his dad.

"Hey, Dad." They give each other the half-hug, half-backslap.

"Son, you look well." He looks at me and smiles. "Introduce us to your girl."

Jack holds his hand out to me. "Guys, this is Harley. Harley, this is my father, Jerry, and my mother, Kim."

I hold out my hand to his dad first. "It's so nice to meet you both." Jerry doesn't take it—instead he gives me a big hug, which surprises me and makes me feel all warm inside. Jack's mom smiles warmly at me but seems a little distant.

They only had carry-on luggage, and we're able to make our way out to the parking lot right away. I shouldn't have come because they're all catching up and I feel awkward just standing here saying nothing. Luckily Charlie wants to hold my hand while we make our way outside.

In Jack's SUV I sit in back with Jack's mom, and Charlie sits between us chattering happily to her nana. We head to Delilah and Reece's place first. While they have their reunion, I excuse myself with the explanation that I need to check on some stuff at home.

Once I make my escape, I'm able to breathe a little better. I know why his mom isn't warming up to me right away. She, I'm sure, watched her son struggle dealing with the shit that his ex-wife had pulled, and Kim probably just wants to make sure I'm not crazy like Becky.

To be honest, watching the little family reunion made my heart hurt a little bit. I'll never have that—no family coming to visit me, or coming to check and make sure I'm doing okay.

"Stop the pity party, Harley," I whisper.

I walk through my house, straightening up a little bit before grabbing a glass of water. I swear I'm out of shape.

I *did* start doing yoga again, but I need to listen to my body. I get back up and grab some more clothes, but maybe I should just stay here. His parents are staying at his place and I don't want it to be awkward.

In my office I open my bottom desk drawer, sighing when I spot what I was looking for. I haven't looked at the photo album of my family in over a year. Usually I have a bottle of wine nearby as I look at pictures and cry.

Watching Jack's parents hug him and Charlie, and then seeing the big reunion when we got to Del and Reece's house...it all made my chest hurt and filled me with envy. Of course that is so wrong and makes me feel guilty, but do they know just how *lucky* they are?

I carry the photo album into the living room and sit down on the couch. Do I look and reopen that wound? A knock on the door stops me, and I set the book down on the couch. I look out the window and find Jack's mom at the door.

Pulling it open, I smile. "Hi, Mrs. Mackenzie. I started straightening up, and just kind of went a little nuts." I laugh, and when I'm nervous I tend to go high-pitched.

She steps inside. "Harley, please call me Kim. I just wanted to apologize because I know I was a little standoffish earlier. He and Becky were together a long time ago, but it hurt me to watch him—first when they started fighting all of the time, then when he wanted us to have custody of Delilah and Becky threatened to take her away from all of us.

"Jack has a lot of regrets, and I hated seeing my son hurt," she continues. "But I can tell he cares about you a lot. Delilah and Reece have told us so many good things about you. I guess I just needed to see what you were like for myself."

"I get it, and I'd like to say I'm the type of person that doesn't need anyone's approval, but I won't lie, I appreciate your words."

Kim pulls me into a hug. "You *don't* need my approval. Now, my son says you write romance novels. I run a bookstore and love to read romance. Can I see your books?"

Now *books* I can talk about all day long. I take her back to my office and show her each of my titles. Kim says she's going to order some copies for the bookstore, and she buys my first series off Amazon for her Kindle. I'm nervous and warn her that my books are graphic in the sex department.

"Oh...*perfect*, something to spice things up in the bedroom." She winks at me and I swear my face turns red like a tomato. "Come on, let's go next door."

I lead her outside and lock the door behind me. She loops her arm through mine, and we walk across our driveways.

When we step inside, Jack comes to me immediately. "Are you okay?"

"Yes, of course. I just wanted to give you a little time. Plus I just needed to check on things. Your mom bought some of my books." I look at him and smile. "She's also going to buy copies for the store—that's so awesome."

Jack wraps his arms around me. "That's great, baby." With his arm around my shoulders, we join the others.

***

I help Kim carry in the balloon bouquets, the flowers, and the rest of the decorations. Jack and his dad have my car and are picking up all of the food.

This afternoon is Del's baby shower. We've been up since seven and have been going nonstop. Jack and his dad got into an argument earlier about who was paying for it all. In the end, Jack conceded and let his dad pay, but he was *not* happy about it.

Things have been going really well since his parents have been here. It felt really awkward going to bed with Jack knowing that his parents were right down the hall. Needless to say, I've thwarted all of his sexual advances and it's been so hard.

This morning I'd woken to his head between my legs and had to put my pillow over my head to muffle my moans when I began to come. Then I *had* to return the favor and blow him until he shot his load down my throat.

"Harley?"

Kim pulls my attention back to her. "Sorry, I was in my own little world there for a second." I set the bags of decorations on the couch next to the balloon bouquets and turn to her. "You tell me what to do—I've never decorated for a party before."

"Really?" She gives me a look I don't understand, but I ignore it.

We spend the next couple of hours decorating Jack's place until it is absolute perfection. We decided on a baby jungle animal theme for the upcoming addition to the Meyers family. The men have been in the kitchen prepping the burgers and hot dogs they're going to grill. It's so funny watching them work together.

Jerry is hilarious and loves giving his son shit, but Jack gives it right back. "My boys have always been like that," Kim explains. "When Jackson was in high school, we hit those hormonal years, and Lord help me, those two fought *all* of the time. But Jack grew out of that phase, thankfully. Do you have any siblings?"

I shake my head. "No. I mean, I have a brother, but I haven't seen him in a very long time. He was not a good person."

"I'm sorry. What about the rest of your family?"

"Umm...well, my mom died when I was five. My dad couldn't handle it, so he dumped my brother and me with our grandma. I haven't seen him since. My brother is a criminal, and could be in jail or dead for all I know. I've been on my own since my grandma passed away when I was eighteen." I avoid looking at her while I tie a green ribbon around the little bag of colored M&M's.

Kim places her hand on my arm. "It takes a lot of strength to keep taking hits like that and to keep getting back up." She reaches out and brushes a strand of hair out of my face. My eyes begin to burn and I blink back the tears that want to escape.

"Thank you for saying that. I don't always feel strong." She squeezes my hand, giving me a reassuring smile.

"What's going on?" I turn to find Jack standing in the opening of the kitchen, his brow furrowed as he takes us both in.

Kim sighs. "Oh Jackson, relax. We were just talking." She looks at her phone and then back at me. "It's probably time to get ready. Reece's parents should be here soon with the cake." She disappears upstairs.

I need to do the same, and I head up to Jack's bedroom. I throw on a pair of worn denim capris, a black ribbed tank top, and a royal blue cardigan. After brushing my hair, I'm just putting my hair in a braid when Jack comes in.

"Hey honey, is the food all ready?"

He wraps his arms around me. "Yep, the grill is ready to go too." Jack kisses my neck. "Thank you for helping with this today."

"I'm happy to do it. I love your family." It's the truth; they're sweet people.

Jack turns me in his arms. "I—*fuck*, I don't know how to say this." Oh God, is he dumping me right before the party? He scrubs his hand over his head. "I thought I was falling in love with you, but the truth is I love you...there, I said it. I love you." He blows out a breath.

No man has ever said that to me. My heart swells. My mouth opens and closes, but no sound comes out. In my head I'm screaming the words back at him. Instead, I do the only thing I can think of to show him I feel the same way.

I grab him by his face, pulling him down until I can reach his lips. I kiss him with everything I have. Jack takes over the kiss, forcing my mouth open and thrusting his tongue inside. I wrap my arms around his shoulders and he lifts me until my legs are wrapped around his hips.

He carries me through his room until my back is against the wall. The doorbell ringing causes us to stop. Jack rests his forehead against mine, and a giggle slips past my lips. He kisses me quickly.

"I'll go downstairs and help them finish up," I tell him. Jack sets me down on my feet. I wrap my arms around his waist, giving him a quick squeeze.

"I'll be down in a minute."

Downstairs, I find both Reece's and Jack's parents in the kitchen. "Harley, these are Reece's parents, Elizabeth and Rich. This is Jack's girlfriend, Harley."

Reece looks like his dad, and his mom is beautiful. They both stand up to greet me and seem very nice. She shows me the cake and it's so cute: It's a jungle scene with fondant animals.

Jack joins us a few minutes later, and then everyone starts to arrive. Del and her family arrive first, and it is chaos while hugs and kisses are exchanged. Then other guests start to arrive, and I get to meet Del's best friend Brandon and his husband, Jose. Erik and Egan come with their wives and kids.

The only person that didn't come was Reece's sister, Rachel. Her oldest is sick and they didn't want to risk getting anyone else sick. We decided against games, but Jerry did get bubbles and chalk to keep the kids occupied.

The men all gather around the grill like they've never seen meat cooked before. I walk around refilling or getting everyone drinks, trying to be a good hostess. I've never thrown a party before, so I want to make sure that everyone is having fun.

I step outside. "Do you boys need a beer?"

Erik wraps his arm around my shoulders. "What are you doing with this old man?"

"His mom is paying me," I say dryly. He barks out a laugh.

"Jack, she's quick. She's going to keep you on your toes."

My man looks at me and winks.

"Jack, did you just *wink* at her?" Reece shakes his head. "I don't think I've *ever* seen you wink before." The men all start razzing him, and he takes it all in stride.

On that note, I head inside.

Chapter Seventeen

Jack

I hold the door open to the coffee shop and follow my parents inside. I wanted Harley to come with to take my parents to the airport, but she got edits back so she was in my office when we left working on them. My mom cracked up and took pictures of Fifty asleep on his little bed on my desk.

Surprisingly, my dad loved the bunny and was always holding him. Fifty was my dad's buddy in the mornings when he'd sit outside drinking his coffee—forever snoozing in my dad's lap.

The hostess seats us. "I wish Harley would've been able to come," my mom says with a smile as she slides into the booth.

"I know, and she wanted to come, but she said she usually has a short amount of time to work on her edits before she has to send them back." We order our coffees. "Do you guys think you'll be able to come back up when Delilah has the baby?"

"We're definitely going to try." My mom

reaches across the table and grabs my hand. "We really like Harley. I love the way she looks at you, the way she treats you, and the way she is with Delilah and the kids."

Our waitress interrupts us to bring our coffee and take our orders. When she walks away, I look at my parents. "I think she's the one. I know I always swore that I'd never go through with getting married again, but she makes me want to."

My mom gives a little squeal; I can only shake my head. "Your mom's happy, if you couldn't tell," my dad chimes in. "I'm happy for you, son. We're just happy that you didn't let the she-devil completely ruin you."

My dad refuses to ever say my ex-wife's name. When we first got divorced, my dad referred to her as "the fucking whore," "the she-bitch," and other names that I don't care to repeat—no matter how much I hate her, she's still Delilah's mother.

After we finish eating, we head to the airport. My parents have me drop them off curbside in front of the gate for the airline they're using. I hop out, wrapping my arms around my mom when I reach her. She sniffles and I know she's crying. "How about once Delilah has the baby Harley and I come down to see you?"

"Oh, that would be wonderful. She's never seen the ocean." I know Harley and my mom bonded during this visit, which makes me glad since Harley's mom is gone. Mom kisses both my cheeks. "Take care of my babies for me, and you call me the minute my great-grandson is born."

"I will, promise. I love you."

Mom lets go so I can hug my dad. "Take care of yourself, old man."

"You too, son, and give Harley our love." I watch as my dad grabs my mom's hand and they make their way toward the doors.

Airport security gives me a look, so I hop in my SUV and then head to the office. Cobi's meeting me to discuss some information he's discovered about the couple whose IP address was used by *Martha*.

After I pull into the parking garage, I hop out and make my way up. Carrie greets me when I step off the elevator. "Good morning, Jack."

"Hey, darlin'. How are you?"

She stands up and runs a hand over a barely there bump. "We're having another baby."

I come around and give her a huge hug. "That's wonderful news. What does Leif think about being a big brother?" Their son is just a few months older than Charlie.

"He wants the baby out now so they can play, and Egan's over the moon." Carrie smiles up at me.

"I'm sure he is." I kiss her cheek and then head into the back.

Cobi is sitting in my office when I step inside. I sit down. "I appreciate you staying in Indy and doing more digging. Is Sara really Martha?"

He opens the folder in front of him. "Sara's father is the pastor at the church they attend. Her father is the one that introduced her to Justin when he joined their congregation six years ago. I attended a service as someone looking for a new church and used my charm…had some of the female parishioners *very* eager to share information with me."

"What we really need is to get into their home and look on their computer," I mutter. "If either one of them are the ones sending the emails, we could find the proof we need. I need to see how friendly they are, or if they're willing to invite a new member of their flock to their home."

"When I was there, a few of the ladies introduced me to them and Justin is a Colts fan. I was able to talk out of my ass enough that he thinks we have a shared interest. I'll go back this weekend and see if I can get an in."

I flip through the papers in the file. Cobi got lots of information—he's been a real asset to our team. The guy's a chameleon, able to assimilate into any situation. "I appreciate it. Make sure you save all of your receipts and Shayla can make sure you get reimbursed for it."

Cobi gets up and walks out of my office. I grab my phone and call Harley to check in on her.

"Hey, honey. Did your parents get off okay?"

"Yeah, they did. How are edits going?" A message pops up on my computer screen, grabbing my attention. "Babe, can I call you back?"

I hang up and head down the hall to Dalton's office. "What the fuck happened to you?" He's sporting a black eye and a split lip.

"Bloody hell...we were only sparring and she got pissed when I insulted her technique. She went ballistic and started trying to *really* fight me. They may ask me to step down, but I wanted you to know." Dalton picks up an ice pack from his desk and places it on his face.

"I'll have Marcus talk to the coach and try to smooth things over."

"Thanks, boss."

Back in my office, I go over the reports of cases my team's been working on. I trust my crew to take care of business, but I just like to keep aware of everything.

***

I grip Harley's hips hard enough to leave bruises, but she's got me so hot right now that if I don't come soon, I will literally die. She moans, cries, and babbles incoherently. The wet sound of her pussy as I pound into her echoes through our room. I love how wet I can make her and how responsive she is.

"You're squeezing my dick so hard. Are you going to come again?" Harley moans and thrusts back hard against me. "Oh yeah, you're going to fucking come, aren't you?"

I reach around and begin strumming her clit. I feel it as she begins to come again. I grab her, pulling her up so her back is against my front and I begin thrusting up into her. I grab her by a chunk of hair and tilt her head to the side.

I bite into her neck and in no time I begin coming violently. I hold onto her because I'm sure I'm close to blacking out. When the feeling fades, I kiss the side of her neck, pulling my softening cock from her. "Let me get rid of the condom. I'll be right back."

I pull the rubber off as I step across the hall to the bathroom. Quickly, I clean up and then head back into the bedroom. Harley is lying on her side under the covers, watching me. Lifting the covers, I slide in next to her and pull her into my arms.

In the dark I hold her to my chest; I close my eyes and enjoy the feel of her in my arms. "Jack?"

"Yeah, baby?"

She snuggles in closer. "I've been thinking a lot lately, and I was wondering if you'd find my dad for me."

My body stiffens—what do I do? If I tell her yes and pretend to do it and she finds out I already knew, she'll be pissed. But if I tell her right now I already did, she'll be pissed. I'm just going to bite the bullet and do it. She'll forgive me when I tell her what I found and why I kept it to myself...I hope.

"I need to tell you something, and I need you to listen to me before you say anything. I wanted to do something for you after that shit I pulled when I pushed you away. I decided to look for your dad." She stiffens next to me. "I found him."

She sits up in bed, and even in the dark I can feel her eyes on me. "Tell me what you found." Harley's voice sounds devoid of any emotion.

I turn on the lamp next to the bed and push myself up to rest against the headboard. "He lives downtown. He works at a realty company." I scrub my face with my hands. "He's married and...and you have a half-sister."

"How old is she?" Harley wraps her arms around herself.

"Twenty-five."

Before I can stop her, she's up and out of bed,

running out of the bedroom and into the bathroom. I jump out of bed and follow her, but when I try to open the door, I find that it's locked. "Harley? Come on baby, let me in."

I put my ear to the door, but hear nothing. I knock lightly. "Baby, let me in." I hear a muffled cry coming through the door, and my heart aches. I want to break the damn door down and stop her tears. "Fuck me, I'm so sorry, Harley. That man doesn't deserve your tears. He was a coward who abandoned his family when they needed him most."

For an hour I sit on the floor in the hallway and listen to her cry, feeling like a helpless asshole. The door finally opens and I get up off the floor. My hip doesn't like that and it takes me a minute to shake out the stiffness.

"Tomorrow, you're going to take me to him." Her voice is still flat and lifeless.

A part of me wants to laugh because the whole time we're dealing with this we're both naked, but instead I freeze. "You want me to take you to him?"

"Yes, you found him and you're going to take me to see him. I want answers—I want to know why he left."

I'd really like to talk her out of it, but if I don't take her, she'll go on her own. "Okay, baby. I'll take you tomorrow."

She nods and crawls into bed, pulling the covers up to her neck and closing her eyes. I climb in and shut off the lamp. Thankfully she lets me pull her into my arms. It's a long time before I feel her finally relax, and only then do I allow myself to fall asleep.

***

Harley's quiet and has been since we got up this morning. I know she's upset with me, and I deserve her anger or her hurt. Honestly, I thought I was helping and doing something good—I should've just told her from the beginning.

I park my SUV down the street from the office the man works at. I called this morning before we left the house, making sure that her dad would be in the office. Harley's leg bounces up and down rapidly, and she wrings her hands together.

I reach over, grabbing her face with both hands, making her look at me. "We don't have to do this. We can go home right now."

Harley shakes her head. "No, I need to do this or it's going to eat at me."

We climb out, and at least she lets me grab her hand as we walk toward the doors. I pull it open and let her pass through first. The receptionist looks up as we walk toward her. "May I help you?"

"We're looking to speak with Randall Sanders, please," I tell her. Nervous energy vibrates from Harley and I wrap my arm around her shoulders, hugging her into my side.

"Is he expecting you?"

"No, he's not." I hope that doesn't stop them from letting us see him.

The receptionist picks up the phone. "Mr. Sanders, are you available? I have new clients who've come in to speak to you." She listens to whatever is being said and then hangs up. "You can go on back. His office is the third door on the left."

We head into the back. "You say the word and we're gone, okay?" I whisper to her.

Harley nods, but keeps walking.

We reach his office and I knock on the doorframe. "Hello, how can I help you?" he asks, looking at me. When he turns to Harley, his face pales. "H-Harley? Is that you?" Randall walks toward her, but Harley holds up her hand, stopping him. "You're so beautiful."

"Shut up," she whispers harshly. "You *left* us and started another family while I lost *everyone*. While you've been enjoying your new life I've been alone, afraid to truly let myself get close to people because the people I love kept leaving me." Harley's face is flushed, and her eyes are bright with unshed tears.

"If you'd let me just explain...sweetheart, things were so hard after your mom died." Again the man tries to move toward her, but she backs away.

Harley looks at me. "I don't know why I did this. This man is no longer my father." She turns and rushes out of the office.

Randall looks at me and I can see the grief on his face. "I know I don't deserve it, but I'd love to be able to explain why I did what I did. Can you talk to her for me?"

I shake my head. "No. If she decides to talk to you, it'll be because she came to that decision herself, and we'll be in touch. If she doesn't, that's her choice."

He nods, looking defeated, and then I walk out of his office and out of the building. I find Harley leaning against my SUV. "I'm so sorry."

She holds up her hand, her face showing so much sadness. "I know you were trying to do something nice, but don't ever do something like that behind my back again. I wasn't ready for this shit."

I pull her into my arms, hugging her tightly. "You're right, and I'm sorry. I seriously thought I was doing a good thing, but then when I found out you had a half-sister, I didn't know what to do."

We stop for lunch before we head home, but she only picks at her food. I reach across the table and grab her hand. "That man doesn't deserve you. He had nothing to do with the strength that you have: That's all you. Since I've known you, I've seen that you're compassionate, giving, loving, and I could really go on and on. It's why I fell in love with you." Her eyes turn bright again. "If you decide you want to give him the time to explain, I'll support you. I'll stay by your side for whatever you need."

"Thank you, Jack," she says quietly.

Chapter Eighteen

Harley

It's been a week since I've seen my dad. After doing a lot of thinking and talking to Jack's mom on the phone, I've decided that right now I don't really want to talk to him. Nothing he can say will make me forgive him for what he did. How do you abandon your children when they need you most, but turn around and start a new family not even two years later?

I've forgiven Jack for looking for my dad and not telling me right away, and I get why he did. He just wasn't expecting to find that my dad had gotten remarried and had another child—a child I don't ever care to know.

In the midst of all of that, Martha sent me another gift. Delilah had seen it get delivered, so she called us and Jack went to get it. She sent me a Bible with so many passages highlighted. All of them were centered around sin, sex, and punishment.

Jack took it to have it fingerprinted, and they took everything they had from Martha to a buddy of his on the police force. He was going to talk to someone at the Indy police force and see if they had enough evidence to bring Sara and Justin in for at least some questioning.

Last I knew, Jack was still waiting to hear back from their contact at the police department. I don't dare admit that I'm scared. Before when it was just emails, I could handle that—just imagining that it was some keyboard warrior. But that was before the shredded book, and a Bible, and before someone made me wreck my car.

Jack has been so amazing; I know he's got his team working round the clock trying to find out who Martha truly is, but it's like she's a ghost. A part of me thinks that eventually Martha will go away, but then it reminds me of books I've read where the women think they're safe and the next thing you know, they're kidnapped or hurt at the hands of the bad guy.

While I watch *Shameless* on Netflix, I make goodie bags for my signing downtown this coming weekend. In each bag is a pen with my logo, a ChapStick, and some candy. For the people who pre-ordered books, they get goodie bags, a tumbler with my logo on it, and a cute little tote bag with my books on it.

Jack is coming with me as my "assistant"—he's just worried and protective, but I'm surprising him with a stay in one of the hotel's swanky suites instead of a regular room. I already told him that people may take his picture because he *does* look like he could be a cover model. He just shook his head and then kissed me.

Once I'm finished with all of the goodie bags, I put them in the big crafts container I have that goes on a little wheelie cart that makes it all easy to move. I grab all of my pre-order books and start signing them and putting them in a separate container from the books that I'll have available for purchase.

I move all of my stuff into the corner of Jack's dining room since we don't really use it. I grab Fifty out of his cage and snuggle him to my chest. "How's my baby? Are you Mommy's sweet boy?" He loves when I scratch under his chin. I swear he's got cat in him somewhere, because he leans into his scratches like a cat would.

In the refrigerator I grab him some greens and we go outside, where I let him sit on the deck while he eats his snack. When he's done I carry him back inside, letting him hop around while I quickly clean his cage. Then I gently place him back in.

Yawning widely, I head upstairs and collapse on the bed, falling asleep almost as soon as I get snuggled up.

"Harley." I feel fingers touch my face, and I slap them away. "Baby, wake up." Opening my eyes, I smile when I find Jack sitting next to me on the bed.

"Sorry, I was so tired." I yawn and cover my mouth with the back of my hand. "How was your day?"

"It was good, baby. I brought home Popeye's. Does that sound good?"

My stomach chooses that moment to growl—

loudly. "My stomach says it does." Jack helps me out of bed and leads me downstairs. I sniff the air and moan. "You got me the spicy, didn't you?"

"I did. Come sit and I'll make you a plate." I sit at the kitchen table and he brings me a plate full of fried chicken, mashed potatoes, red beans and rice, and a biscuit. He then sets a beer down in front of me.

"Thanks, baby. You take such good care of me."

He bends down and kisses my lips. "It's my honor to do it."

Jack joins me at the table with a plate fuller than mine. We're both too busy shoveling our food into our mouths, but it's always a comfortable silence with us.

After we finish, I wrap up the leftovers so he can take his lunch to work tomorrow.

While he watches the Cubs play, I lie on the other end of the sectional and read an ARC I got from an author friend of mine.

***

The hot water cascades over my body and I close my eyes, letting it loosen up my tense muscles. This afternoon we're heading downtown to the Hyatt for the book signing for tomorrow. I've made us reservations at this great sushi restaurant and steakhouse. It's my way of thanking him for everything he's done for me.

After washing my body and my hair, I rinse off and then step out of the shower. I wrap my towel around myself and use the other towel on my hair.

After I'm done, I rub some leave-in conditioner in my hair and comb it through.

Jack's at the office this morning, which is good. It gives me time to get ready without him distracting me with his sexiness. I take my towel off and toss it on the bed. I grab one of my new bra and pantie sets and slip them on.

My stomach starts to roll and I make a run for the bathroom. I make it to the toilet just as I throw up over and over. When I finish, I stand up and rinse my mouth out. "Damn nerves." I throw on my robe and quickly put some makeup on.

After drying my hair, I add some loose waves to it. I throw on some black leggings, a white tank top, and a slouchy off-the-shoulder t-shirt. I slip on my Converse, and then I pull my outfit out for dinner later tonight.

For the signing I'm wearing black capris with a white button-up shirt; Delilah helped me pick out some really cool jewelry to wear with it. Yesterday I surprised Delilah, Shayla, and Carrie with general admission tickets to the signing.

I hear the front door opening. "Harley?"

"Up here."

Jack comes walking into the bedroom. "Damn you look sexy, baby."

I roll my eyes and he charges me. I squeal and he tackles me to the bed. He climbs on top of me, shackling my wrists above my head with one hand. "Hmmm...should I tickle you?" Jack runs his fingers down my side, making me squirm.

"*Nooo*...don't. We've got to get ready to go, you big oaf."

"*Oaf?* That's it." He tickles me until I'm squirming and squealing, but a wave of nausea hits me again.

"Get off…get off…*get off*." Jack scrambles off of me, and I rush off the bed and into the bathroom, bending over the toilet just in time.

I feel his hand on my back. "Baby, are you okay?" I nod, and he helps me stand up. He hands me a wet washcloth to wipe off my mouth.

"Yeah, it's just nerves."

Jack's quiet for a moment. "When was your last period?"

"Last month, and I'm due to start next week." I can tell he's starting to freak out. "I have a nervous stomach. I'm *not* pregnant, so you can stop freaking out."

"I'm *not* freaking out." He follows me out of the bathroom and into the bedroom. "Harley, you could still be pregnant. It might be too early to tell."

"Jack, it was one time without a condom." I shake my head. "Is *this* where you run scared? I realize your ex-wife screwed you over, but I'm not her. Plus I told you I don't really want kids." That lie is beginning to slide off the tongue too easily.

He moves toward me. "I *know* you're not my ex. A million times over you're not my ex. If I were ever to have more children, I'd want you to be their mother." Jack grabs me by my shoulders. "I mean it. If I decided to have more children, I'd want them with you."

My heart beats wildly in my chest at his words. "Okay, but I'm not pregnant."

He shakes his head. "I'm going to change and

pack." Jack kisses me roughly before letting me go.

***

Jack pulls out my seat for me and then takes the one across from me. He was excited when I told him we were going to eat at Roka Akor for dinner, and he looks so handsome in his black dress slacks and blue button-up shirt with his sleeves rolled up.

I'm wearing a black form-fitting dress that hits me right above my knee, a red blousy shrug, and black heels. My hair is up in a bun on top of my head. He tried to get me naked before we left, but I managed to fend him off.

Our waiter comes and we order drinks. I order water and a blood orange margarita. Jack orders a beer. "Are you excited for tomorrow?" he asks.

"Excited *and* nervous. I feel so awkward when I try to sell my books. Did Del tell you I got tickets for her, Shayla, and Carrie to come?" I play with the napkin in my lap.

"She did. That's really sweet of you to do that."

"I *am* pretty sweet," I say, giving him what I hope is a saucy grin. Our waiter stops at our table to bring our drinks and take our orders.

When dinner is over, I have a nice little buzz going. We ordered some warm chocolate cake to take back to the hotel and preferably eat naked in bed.

We enter the Hyatt, which is gorgeous, and hand in hand we make our way to the elevators. On our way, I bump into a man. "Oh gosh, I'm sorry," I say.

The look he throws me gives me pause, but then he hurries off in the opposite direction.

"Harley?"

I turn to look at Jack. "I just ran into some guy and I don't think he liked it."

The elevator opens and he pulls me on, wrapping his arms around me. His lips are on mine as the doors slide shut.

***

Jack helps me set up my table, and by *help*, I mean he helped me bring my stuff downstairs. A couple of authors come over and introduce themselves to me and we talk while I arrange stuff on my table.

Once I'm done, we head back upstairs so I can change into the outfit I'm wearing. I decide to wear the black ballet flats today because last night I'd pushed it a little bit wearing heels. But it was so worth it when we got back to our room last night and Jack had me bent over the mattress—with the heels on, I was at the perfect height.

My body heats up as I think about it, but I push that away to get changed. When I'm finished, I head back out into the little living room. Jack looks up when I walk in. "You look amazing."

"Thank you."

Once we get downstairs, it's a whirlwind of activity. We do a group photo, and then I ask the author next to my table to take mine and Jack's picture. While I get myself organized, Jack grabs us both a bottle of water.

"What do we do now?" He wraps his arm around the back of my chair.

I shrug. "Now we pretty much just wait for it to start." I lean into Jack. "If you want to go sit in the bar or upstairs until it starts, that's fine with me. I don't want you getting bored."

"Well, I wanted to come and support you, so how could I be bored? I'm excited to see my girl in action." He wraps his arm around me and kisses my temple.

When they announce that the doors are opening, the place is suddenly really loud and busy. My stomach rolls, but I swallow the bile down and pop a peppermint into my mouth. As people begin stopping by my table, Jack becomes the best helper. He poses for pictures, takes pictures for me, and shoots the breeze with husbands and boyfriends who were dragged there by their partners.

What surprises me the most is when he starts talking to a girl's husband who just stopped to look at the covers of my books. Jack gives the guy a full-blown marketing pitch and he ends up buying his wife my complete series.

The girls show up with Erik in tow, and they pose for pictures with me. Then Shayla takes a picture of Del, Jack, and me. They all buy books from me and I sign them. I've never had close friends like this before—it feels good.

Jack looks at his phone and signals to Erik. They look at the screen together and then Jack comes over to me. "I'll be right back." He and Erik disappear out into the lobby.

I look at the girls. "What was that about?" The

three of them shrug. "Will you guys sit and watch my table while I go use the bathroom?"

"Of course," Shayla says as the three of them sit down.

I run out the side door to the bathroom that sits across from the main entrance. I quickly use the facilities and then wash my hands. In the mirror, I glance at my reflection and realize I look...*different.* I look happy—content. I smile like a goon—I know, I just can't help it.

Smiling, I reach for the handle of the door and pull it open. I let out a squeak because a man is standing in the doorway. "Umm...this is the ladies room."

With quick movements, he shoves me back inside. I lose my balance and fall, hitting the wall on my way down. He grabs me and pulls me up to my feet. My body shakes from fear—I don't know who this man is, or what I did.

He leans in close so I can smell his rancid breath. "I told you that you'd be punished."

My eyes widen as I struggle to find words, get my body to move...*anything. Oh God, it can't be.*

"I caught my wife with one of your books, and I read that piece of whorish trash," he snarls. "You should be ashamed of yourself." His hand flies out and he slaps me across the face. Pain explodes in my cheek as I whimper and cover it with my hand.

I vaguely recall Jack and Egan telling me to respond to *Martha's* emails by apologizing. This man is out of his mind, but I'll gladly agree with him if it'll save my life. "Y-Yes, you're-you're right," I whisper, and I don't have to fake the wobble in my voice. "I'm sorry."

"You're *sorry*?" He grabs me by the shoulders and slams me into the wall. "You're a *whore*, and God punishes whores. 1 John 1:9: 'If we confess our sins, he is faithful and just to forgive us our sins and to cleanse us from all unrighteousness.' It's too late for you to repent now. It's time for me to punish you for your sins."

It's so fast I don't even have time to react—the pain is hot and blinding, and I fall to my knees. I look up as he pulls the knife from my gut and sneers at me before he kicks me in the ribs. Then in a flash, he's gone.

My hands tremble and my legs wobble as I push myself up to stand. I clamp my hands over my stomach and feel the warm blood flowing between my fingers.

I feel like I'm about to pass out, but I force myself to take one step at a time. I need to get to Jack. I open the door as the tears start to flow down my cheeks. I use the wall for support as I step out into the hall. "O-One f-foot…in front of…the o-other," I whisper.

My vision swims and I fight the urge to collapse.

More blood seeps through my fingers…it feels like so much. My vision tunnels, but I force myself to take step after step. I open the door to the event hall and propel myself through it. Each step is getting harder and harder…I start coughing and it tastes metallic, causing my stomach to roil.

I hear someone yell, and then my name is being called. I look up and see Erik and Jack. Jack's head whips in my direction and his eyes widen before he comes running toward me. My legs can no longer hold me up and I drop to the floor.

Jack appears above me. I can see his lips moving, but I can't hear him. I open my mouth: *"I love you."* I'm not sure if any sound comes out, and finally my eyes flutter shut.

Chapter Nineteen

Jack

Erik and I step out into the hall. Cobi's been blowing up my phone—hopefully he's got information for me. "What's up, Cobi—do you have news?"

"Jack, it's the husband," he blurts. "I broke into their house to get on the computer and I found Sara beaten—she was barely conscious. He's there, Jack—he's going to make his move."

Without a word, I hang up and turn to Erik. "Martha's a guy—it's a *man* that's been messing with Harley. He beat his wife and then he came here." My phone dings and it's a text from Cobi with a picture of Justin. I show it to Erik. "This is the guy; keep an eye out."

We rush back into the event hall and we're a foot from Harley's table when I hear commotion and look to the side. In all my life, I will *never* forget the moment that I see the love of my life holding her stomach with blood dripping from between her fingers, staining her shirt, and coating her lips.

I bark at Erik to call 9-1-1 while I run to Harley. "Baby, stay with me...we're getting help." Her eyes keep fluttering closed. "*Harley*, stay with me!"

Shayla gets on the floor next to me, holding her sweater to Harley's stomach wound. Carrie, Delilah, and some others keep people back. It feels like forever before the paramedics finally show up. They get her on the stretcher and I ask Carrie, Shayla, Del, and Erik to get my and Harley's stuff together.

They let me ride in the ambulance with her, and I'm barely aware of what they're saying—my eyes are only on her, my mind is only on her. We finally reach Rush Hospital and they make me go out to the waiting room while they rush her into triage.

I pace back and forth after texting Erik and letting them know where we are. I look down at my hands that are covered in blood—*Harley's* blood—and they begin to tremble. Clenching my fists, I stare blindly out the window.

I'm not sure how much time has passed, but I sip at the bitter, disgusting brew that my daughter brought me a while ago. It sits like acid in my gut.

"She's going to be okay," Delilah says as she hugs my waist. I nod and wrap my arm around her shoulders, hugging her to my side.

My whole team is here waiting. Cobi feels like shit and keeps apologizing for not making a move earlier, but this motherfucker was really good at hiding how evil he truly is.

Luckily someone was watching over us, because hotel security saw Justin on tape. The guy obviously has never done something like this before because he drove his *own* car, and security was able to get the make and model as well as the plates.

The last update I heard was that the guy wrecked his car running from the cops. He's not at this hospital—otherwise I would probably try to kill him. At this point, they don't know if he's even going to make it, and after what he did to Harley and his own wife…if that motherfucker dies, then he'll be getting off too easy.

"Harley Sanders's family?" I turn to the doors that lead into the back. A man in scrubs is standing there.

I jump up. "Yes, that's us." He leads Delilah and me through the doors.

"I'm Dr. Torres, and I've been treating Harley. I'm not sure if she's got a guardian angel or what, but the blade missed every vital organ. We closed her up and started IV antibiotics. We're going to keep her overnight to make sure that infection doesn't set in, but you're welcome to stay. I'll send someone once we get her admitted." He disappears down the hall.

"Dad? That's great news." I turn to look at Delilah, and then back down the hall.

I nod, but I need to get out of here—I need a second to breathe. I walk past my daughter, out into the waiting room, and past my team. I don't stop walking until I'm at least a block away. I lace my fingers behind my head and squat down, taking a deep breath.

I stand up and run a hand over my head and close my eyes, saying a little prayer of thanks.

"Jack." I open my eyes to find Reece walking toward me. He pulls me into a back-slapping hug. "Del said Harley's going to be okay?"

"Yeah, man. *Fuck,* I've never been so scared in all my life." I look down at my hands and see that I still have dried blood under my fingernails. "I thought she was dead, man. Her eyes closed, her lips were blue, and she was so fucking *pale.*" I look at him. "I'm never letting her get away. She's going to have to accept the fact that I'm going to marry her and give her the babies she says she doesn't want, because she's a terrible liar."

"I'm happy for you, Jack. You're both lucky to have found each other." Reece slaps my back again and we walk back to the hospital, where we find out that they've got Harley settled into her room.

***

Harley hasn't woken up yet, but they have her on heavy pain meds at the moment. The nurse assured me that she was healing while she slept and she wasn't in any pain. Luckily during her surgery they didn't have to give her a blood transfusion—they just pumped her full of saline.

I sent everyone home earlier. Cobi didn't want to leave, but I knew he was itching to check in on Sara. I just hope he's careful with that situation. My mom also called earlier asking about Harley; she offered to come up and help her during her recovery, but I assured her I have it taken care of.

I stand up to stretch and walk around the room to close the curtains, then sit in the little recliner with my feet resting on the end of her bed. I meant what I said to Reece—I'm going to make her my wife and give her at the very least one or two of my babies.

While I listen to the steady beep of her machines and watch the rise and fall of her chest, I think about one of the books she told me she loved; when the heroine was hurt and in the hospital, she woke up to a ring on her finger.

I send Delilah a text asking her to get the ring box that was in my duffel bag and bring it in the morning. I had planned on—or had at least thought about—proposing to Harley after her signing.

Delilah: Really???? Okay either Reece or I will bring it.

Closing my eyes, it isn't long before I fall asleep.

"Jack?" Harley's hoarse voice pulls me from my sleep.

I get up and grab her hand. "Hi, baby. How are you feeling?" I brush her hair out of her face.

"I hurt. I'm thirsty." I get the nurse, letting her know that Harley's awake. She comes in and checks Harley over before disappearing to get her a cup of ice chips. I elevate the head of her bed enough for me to slip ice chips between her lips. "I'm sleepy," she whispers, and I put the head of her bed back down and Harley falls right back asleep.

I don't sleep much through the night. Nurses periodically come in to check her vitals, her IV, and her dressings.

Reece shows up with the ring box; he leaves us

alone and I open it. It's a platinum band with a princess-cut diamond. I grab her left hand and slip it on her ring finger—it fits perfectly.

I stare out the window and shake my head. In a million years I never thought I'd get married again, but she makes me want to do *a lot* of things I said I'd never do.

***

Harley

I open my eyes and stare up at the plain white ceiling of the hospital room. It feels like someone jammed a hot poker in my gut; I can still feel the blade sinking into my flesh. My heart starts to race. "Harley?" Jack appears above me, and I immediately relax. "Are you okay? You were starting to pant, and your heart rate increased."

"Yeah, I was just remembering everything." I lick my chapped lips. God, even exhausted—which I know he is—he's still a beautiful man.

He grabs my hand, bringing it up to his mouth. "He can't hurt you ever again." I can only nod. He says it with so much conviction that I believe him.

Something sparkling on my hand catches my attention, and I bring my hand up to my face. I look at Jack, forgetting all about the pain. "Ummm…did we get engaged?"

He grins. "I've had it for a little bit. I remember you telling me that in one of your books, the heroine got hurt and while she was in the hospital recovering, she woke with the engagement ring on her finger. And I thought, what better way to ask you?" He leans down, holding my hand in his. "What do you say?" He kisses me right over the ring.

My eyes burn. "I thought you didn't want that?"

"I didn't, until you." Jack kisses me on the lips. "Marry me? Please."

I nod, smiling. "Yes, I'll marry you." He kisses me again. "I love you, Jack."

"I love you too, Harley."

***

Two weeks later

I move slowly through Jack's bedroom—or I should say, *our* temporary bedroom. After our little honeymoon we're taking, he's moving into my home and we're making it ours.

I was released from the hospital two days after I was attacked. I'm not sure how I got so lucky since the knife didn't hit any organs. It'll take some time to completely heal, though. Jack's been the one to change my dressing every day, and again, trying to carry me everywhere.

He's been wonderful to me, and when I have nightmares he holds me until I'm able to fall back asleep. Cobi has been a fixture at Jack's—heck, his whole team and the spouses have been over, cooking or bringing food, helping with whatever we need done.

Jack's told me Cobi still feels guilty and that he thinks he let us down. I finally got him to sit down and talk with me, and I made it very clear that no one blamed him for anything. When he's not with us, he's usually looking in on Sara, even though she always refuses to see him.

We did find out the whole story: Sara had bought a paperback copy of *Release You*, and her husband grabbed it from her and read it. He'd slapped her around and then made her stay on her knees praying for hours. Then he began emailing me and digging until he found out more about me.

When I wouldn't respond to his emails, he got pissed. He made his wife watch as he shredded my books.

"Martha" was the name of the preacher's wife at the church Justin had attended as a child. He'd watched his mom be preached to by his father over and over; his father would make them both kneel while he read scripture after scripture.

I guess he'd just finally *snapped*, and beat Sara badly before coming after me. Justin's still in the hospital, but as soon as he's able, they'll transfer him to jail where he'll face multiple charges, including attempted murder.

But now I'm focusing back on today: the day I'm marrying Jack.

Earlier, Delilah braided my hair in one of those thick fishtail braids, sticking flowers throughout my hair. She even did my makeup, giving me a slight glow. I hugged her tightly. "Thank you for doing this."

While she hugged me, she whispered in my ear, "Can I call you Mommy?" We laughed and then she kissed my cheek before disappearing downstairs.

Jack wanted to get married in Vegas, but then I suggested we just do it here because I was still healing, and doing it here meant the kids could be involved too. His parents flew up for the weekend, and his dad had pulled me aside and asked if he could have the privilege of giving me away.

His sweet gesture made me cry, but I was honestly still a bit of an emotional mess.

I've thought about reaching out to my dad, but I'm nowhere near ready for that, and I may never be. If anything, I just want answers and then to move on with my life, with my new family.

Someone knocks, and when the door opens, Jerry sticks his head in the room. "*Wow*, sweetheart, you look beautiful." His smile widens. "I brought someone to help give you away." He's holding Fifty in one hand, and on closer inspection, I see my bunny is wearing a black bow tie. I lean down and kiss his furry head.

"Thank you for giving me away, and thank you for including my little baby." I stand up and brush my hand down the off-white dress with capped sleeves; it has an empire waist so it doesn't rub against the wound on my stomach. The dress is knee-length and I'm wearing a brand-new pair of purple Converses.

"It's my pleasure, beautiful girl." He holds his arm out to me. I loop my arm through his and we head down the steps. Soft classical music plays from the surround sound in the living room. We reach the bottom of the steps and I smile when I see everyone.

As soon as my eyes land on Jack I begin to cry—

happy tears, of course. He smiles widely at me, the smile that I've always loved, especially now that it's directed at me. When we reach him, Jack holds out his hand to me and I take it.

"You look beautiful, baby." He's wearing a white button-up shirt and black dress pants.

In front of our family, I vow to love Jack and spend the rest of my life making him happy. He vows to do the same, and adds that he has something else to say. "When we first met, I admit I wasn't the nicest to you, but that was only because I knew you were going to change my life and I was scared. I'm now grateful every day for you coming into my life—for loving me and my family."

I smile up at him, not even caring that tears are sliding down my face and dripping from my chin.

When the minister announces that we can kiss, Jack grabs my face, kissing me thoroughly until everyone's catcalls cause us to pull away from each other.

Jack's parents ordered appetizers and champagne, which means everyone snacks and everyone who could drink does after the short, sweet ceremony.

Someone turns up the music and "Lucky" by Jason Mraz starts playing through the speakers. My husband grabs me carefully and we begin to slowly dance in the living room. He surprises me by singing along. His voice is deep, rich, and soothing. I rest my cheek on his shoulder and close my eyes.

That's another little tidbit I've learned about my husband: he can sing, and really well too.

When the song ends, I open my eyes and see

everyone is watching us, and they're all smiling.

Reece raises his beer bottle. "To Mr. and Mrs. Mackenzie." I smile at them and then up at Jack. What a perfect day.

Epilogue

Jack

One year later

I pull into the driveway and shut off my SUV. I wave to my grandkids from the front window of their house, then make my way inside the house. Silence greets me. I head down the hall toward our bedroom, where I find my beautiful, heavily pregnant wife fast asleep, wrapped around her body pillow.

Our son Jameson is due any day now, and my girl is hurting. He's a big boy and has been causing her to have lower back pain and hip pain. She can't sleep most of the time.

I sit down next to her and stroke her cheek. Her eyes open and she smiles at me. "You're home."

"How are you feeling?" I help her sit up, and then help her stand.

Harley rubs her hands over her belly. "Tired, sore, and frustrated. Your son doesn't want to come out."

"He'll come when he's ready." I stroke a hand over her hair before leaning down and kissing her lips.

She makes her way into the bathroom. I can hear her fiddling around and then she calls out, "Ummm...Jack? My water just broke." Harley comes waddling out of the bathroom with her dress clearly wet at the bottom.

Harley is cool, calm, and collected, but I begin to panic—rushing around our bedroom and feeling like I don't know what the fuck I'm supposed to be doing. My beautiful, patient wife stops me. "Baby, you have to settle down. I'm good, and hopefully we won't have long to wait before we get to meet our son."

"You're right, sweetheart." I take a deep breath. "I'm good, I promise." I grab her bag and help her get changed into dry clothes so we can head to the hospital.

Once we get there they get us checked in, wheeling her up to labor and delivery, and then I help Harley get changed into her gown. They hook her up to some monitors, and then they start her IV. I send out a group text letting everyone know we're in the hospital and I'll keep them posted as things progress.

We decided we wanted to keep this a private affair—I didn't want her worrying about everyone in her face. I want her to just focus on letting her body do its thing.

Five hours later and Harley's miserable. She wanted to do this au naturel, but the pain became too much so they gave her a shot that would help with the pain and help her relax. She managed to sleep in between contractions, which is what we wanted, her getting some rest. It's now starting to wear off. The nurse said she'd be back soon to check her.

"Baby, you're doing great. Our boy's going to be here soon." I kiss her sweaty forehead.

The nurse pokes her head in the room. "Are we ready to check you to see where you're at?"

Harley nods; she's too tired to talk right now.

Our nurse has Harley bend her legs while she puts her gloves on and then reaches between her legs. "Who's ready to have a baby?" She smiles up at us.

After that, she has Harley push a few times. "That's great, Harley. You're doing really well." I hold Harley's hand as she pushes each time the nurse tells her to. This goes on for about a half hour and then the doctor is coming in.

I wrap my arm around Harley's shoulders and help her lean forward like the nurse instructs us. She smiles at me. "I can see the head. Dad, do you want to look?"

I lean forward and, sure enough, there's a head with dark hair right there. "Baby, I can see our boy. He's almost here."

That encourages her to push harder, and in no time the sweetest sound in the world fills the room: the cries of my son. The doctor has Harley grab the baby under the arms and pull him up onto her chest. Tears fill my eyes as I kiss my wife's sweaty head and smile down at my goo-covered son. "Jack, he's so beautiful."

"That's because you're his momma. God, he's perfect." The nurse takes our son and gets him all cleaned up and then brings him back. She helps Harley place the baby to her breast, and my son knows a good thing when he sees one: He begins nursing right away.

While Jameson nurses, I step into the hall and start making the phone calls. When I'm done, I step back into the room. They've already got the room all straightened up, and Harley in a fresh gown. "Did he eat well?"

"Like a champ. Jameson, do you want your daddy?"

I take my son, holding him in my arms. God, he's fucking beautiful. "Hey buddy, your big sister is on her way to see you. You better be prepared for lots and lots of kisses." He opens his eyes and looks at me and I swear my heart swells.

I can't believe I convinced myself I never wanted any more kids. Jameson is only an hour old and I already can't imagine my life without him in it. It took me twenty-three years to find the right woman to do this with again, and I can't wait to see what our future holds.

***

Harley

Jameson nurses happily while I read in bed. Our little man is a month old already. He's starting to coo when we talk to him and Jack swears he smiled at him, but I didn't have the heart to tell him that it was probably just gas.

This baby is already loved by a lot of people: his big sister, and his niece and nephews. Growing up all I wanted was a huge family to love and one that would love me back. Then as I got older, I kissed that dream goodbye.

Jack just didn't want any part of getting married or having kids again, but together we seemed to fix that for each other. I love that man so much, and every time I look at our son, I love him so much more.

The front door opens and then I hear footsteps. "Daddy's home," I whisper, and sure enough he comes around the corner, looking as handsome as ever. Business for them has been booming, and they've finished the expansion. They've hired some new staff to take on more clients.

Jack has cut down on his hours temporarily, just for the baby's first few months, but he's got a great team and they've stepped in—allowing Jack time with us.

"Hi, babe." He climbs on the bed and kisses me before bending down and kissing our son. "How was he today?"

"Perfect." Once he's done eating, I burp him and then hand him over to Jack.

"I'll change him and then take him out into the living room so you can get some sleep."

He does this every day. It doesn't matter that he was just at work—he wants to do his part. I couldn't have picked a better father for my son. I lie down, hug the pillow to my chest, and smile because life is good.

***

Two years later, it got even better with the birth of our daughter, Gracie.

The End

Sneak Peek

SECURITY DETAIL

*Rogue Security and Investigation Series
Book Four*

Chapter One

Becca

"I have a sparring partner already—why do I need another one? Where's Clint going?" I turn to my longtime coach, Gio.

He hands me a bottle of water. "Because I wanted to switch it up a bit, and this guy is a martial arts expert. He can help you get stronger. The guy's a beast."

I slam my locker shut because I'm pissed. I don't like when things change without me knowing. "Tell me about this guy, or is *that* a surprise too?"

"His name's Dalton Buckley. Like I said, he's an expert. He teaches self-defense to inner-city kids, and he's formerly with the Special Air Service—he's English." Gio writes some shit down in his notebook; he's *always* writing stuff in it. There's something he's not telling me, I just know it.

I sigh. "When do I get to meet this expert?" I don't bother trying to hide the disdain in my voice.

He sets his notebook down. "We're meeting him and his boss today. Be nice to him—he's a good guy. My buddy Marcus is the one that recommended him, and he wouldn't steer us wrong."

After my shower, I change into a pair of black track shorts, my favorite lavender Nike tank top, and my black Nike tennis shoes. I run the brush through my wheat-colored locks and put my hair into a high ponytail.

I head out to Gio's office and take the protein shake he hands me, slamming it down. I swear while I'm training I feel like I eat all day long, but I've got to refuel my body so I can train with the intensity that Gio demands of me.

When I first started fighting I had the worst manager—he took more than what he was entitled to, in more ways than one. My dad fired him immediately but convinced me that I needed to keep what happened quiet; otherwise, it could affect my career.

Yep, my dad was a douchebag and cared more about my career than my well-being. Once I found Gio, I cut all ties with my dad. I just couldn't forgive him. My mom is in the picture, but only when it's photo ops and getting her name in magazines and the papers. I feel like I'm the poster child for dysfunctional families.

Gio hangs up the phone. "Let's go meet your new sparring partner."

We pull up in front of a large office building in his white Navigator. They have a *valet* here? That's crazy. I hop out and stand on the sidewalk waiting for Gio to get out and come around to me. We head inside and go to some elevators in the back.

SECURITY DETAIL

He messes with his phone while I see we've arrived on the floor of Rogue Security and Investigation Inc. "Gio, what the fuck is this? What's going on?"

"Let's head inside and then everything will be explained to you."

At the front desk, a blonde woman sits. She glances up and smiles as we approach. "Can I help you?"

"Yes, we're here to see Jack and Dalton. This is Becca McNeal, and I'm Gio Mendez."

"Of course, Jack's expecting you. Go ahead and head into the back. The conference room is the last door on your right."

ACKNOWLEDGMENTS

First off, thank you to my husband, Jim—thank you for believing in me and my stories. Thank you for always supporting me and loving me.

Thank you to my editor extraordinaire, Sydnee Thompson. Thank you for your hard work making my words even better. I spend most of my time laughing or smiling when I read your comments while working on edits. I've learned a lot since we started working together, and I'm always excited to work with you.

To my girl Angela, thank you for always being there for me. Whether it's while I'm trucking along or riding the struggle bus, you're always there either supporting me or encouraging me. I love your face!!

Diane, my PA, my right-hand man, my rock, you do so much for me I'm not sure how I can ever repay you. You make it so easy for me to focus on writing. I couldn't do it without you.

To the girls in my ARC team, thank you for your never-ending support, for loving my words, and for sharing your love for my stories with others. You guys ROCK!

To everyone at Crave Publishing: You guys make each release so easy, from the gorgeous covers, to the editing, and Lydia's phenomenal marketing. Thank you!

Thank you to my readers for taking a chance on me. I never dreamed this would be my life, but I'm blessed beyond measure!

ABOUT THE AUTHOR

A Midwesterner and self-proclaimed nerd, Evan has been an avid reader most of her life, but five years ago got bit by the writing bug, and it quickly became her addiction, passion and therapy. When the voices in her head give it a rest, she can always be found with her e-reader in her hand. Some of her favorites include, Shayla Black, Jaci Burton, Madeline Sheehan and Jamie Mcguire. Evan finds a lot of her inspiration in music, so if you see her wearing her headphones you know she means business and is in the zone.

During the day Evan works for a large homecare agency and at night she's superwoman. She's a wife to Jim and a mom to Ethan and Evan, a cook, a tutor, a friend and a writer. How does she do it? She'll never tell.

Stay up to date on the latest news.
Be sure to sign up for my newsletter:
https://bit.ly/1RgXn6V

Facebook:
https://www.facebook.com/pages/Evan-Grace/626268640762539

Twitter:
https://twitter.com/Evan76Grace

Website:
http://www.authorevangrace.com/

Goodreads:
https://www.goodreads.com/author/show/7788444.Evan_Grace

Made in the USA
Monee, IL
03 September 2021